LINA
Intangible Touch

ALAIN BOULANGER was born in France and migrated to Australia as a child and eventually settled in Hong Kong. He is the illustrator and editor of the children's book *John The Fish and Other Stories* and the author of the novel *The Shimmer*. This is his second novel.

LINA
Intangible Touch

LINA
Intangible Touch

ZODIAC BOOKS

When you find the right one,
nothing's impossible...

LINA
Intangible Touch

CHAPTER 1

John takes another sip of his whiskey. He hates this feeling. He feels like a sixteen year old school-kid trying to master up the courage to take the few steps across the dance floor to ask a girl for a dance.

He looks up again. She was definitely looking in his direction before her eyes quickly averted his gaze. She has these short blonde hair. They fall down to the base of her neck. He loves short hair. He wonders what it would feel like to kiss her slender neck.

Why is it so hard? It's not like he is ugly or anything. In fact, he would consider himself more on the handsome side. His crew haircut hides some of the white hair that are starting to pepper his head, but he has a nicely shaped head so it suits him anyway. He was told that he has beautiful almond-shaped eyes and that the blue in them seems like a lost ocean. His nose is straight and narrow like a roman statue and his lips are thin. Hitting the gym three times a week has given him a body that turns head at the beach – not the huge, over-inflated type body but the slim, athletic build.

He takes another sip of the whiskey and looks over the rim of his glass. Again, she looks away, he is not sure why. She is so beautiful that she shouldn't have any problems feeling comfortable with herself.

Suddenly she looks up. But this time, when she sees him

looking at her, her eyes stay on him. A little smile crosses her lips, inviting him over. He hesitates for another minute, making sure that she is actually smiling at him and not someone else, then, before he changes his mind, his feet are making their way to her.

"Hi," he says, standing awkwardly next to her, feeling the heat rising to his face – she is even more beautiful from close up.

"Hello," she smiles with a distinctively punctuated 'H' that sounds more like an 'R'. Definitely Russian, he thinks.

" Mmmmmmm...what's...what's your name?" he asks.

"I'm Lina," she replies.

He cannot stop staring at her. He's never talked to anyone that beautiful. She must be a model. Probably she will tell him to piss off in a minute.

"I'm John." He licks his lips nervously.   Errrr...Lina, wow...that's a beautiful name. Are you Russian?"

"Yes," she replies, taking a sip of wine. "I'm from Krasnoyarsk in Russia. Maybe you don't know?"

"Well, I have to admit that I've never heard of that place. Is it close to Moscow?"

She laughs. "No, not close. Far." she blushes. "Mmmmmm...I sorry, my English no so good..."

"No. No, please don't apologize. It's OK, really."

John can feel his knees tremble - why does she make him feel so nervous? He'd better take a seat soon before his knees decide to give up on him. He looks down and sees that the stool next to her is available. "May I?" he asks. He doesn't wait for a reply and settles himself down.

She is smiling at him. She has this beautiful smile and little crow's-feet form at the corner of her eyes. She has these amazing eyes. They are greenish blue with a tint of gray in them. It's hard for John not to keep looking into them. He feels like he could drown in them.

For a minute nothing is said, but the silent is not uncomfortable or awkward. Somehow it feels nice to be seating here next to her and say nothing. She is just smiling at him.

John notices a small, one-inch thin scar running down from the corner of her lower lip. He wonders how she got it. Did she fall down as a child? Did someone hit her? He wants to know more about her.

"Sooooo, you say you're from Russia. What brings you here?" he asks hiding his nervousness with small talk.

"My husband, he has job in bank here, so me also come."

John is taken aback but tries not to show his disappointment - married. Of course she would be married. She is way too beautiful for no one to have noticed.

"Oh, so you are here with your husband?" he makes a show of looking around.

"No, no. He not here, he home."

John feels a sense of relief. He wonders how her husband could feel comfortable letting her go out by herself. He thinks that there is no way that she wouldn't get hit on. If he had a wife that looked like that, there is no way that she would be in a bar by herself. He'd make sure that she'd be right next to him in a warm cozy bed.

"So...how come you are here? I mean, by yourself?" he asks.

"I tell him I go to friend birthday. Birthday finish early and I no want go home. So I come for drink."

John notices her empty glass. He takes his, throws back his head and feels the warm whiskey make its way down. He puts the glass back on the counter and enjoys the numb feeling that's starting to invade his body. He feels good. Who cares if she is married, she is here, for whatever reason, and he's happy to be sitting next to her. The world around him starts to waver and in his mind, there is only the two of them sitting at the bar.

"Mmmmm...I see. Well, I don't mean to sound too forward or anything but, why don't you want to go home?" She doesn't reply straightaway. Maybe that's a bit personal, he realizes. "I'm sorry," he quickly apologizes. "Maybe I shouldn't ask. It's none of my business..."

"No, is OK. My marriage not good. He not nice to me."

He is not sure whether he should intrude or not. Maybe another drink might help them both relax a little...break the ice.

"Can I get you another drink? What are you having?" he asks.

"Yes please," she replies. He sees her shoulders relax – could she be as nervous as he feels? "I like Lemon Drop

3

Martini."

John has never heard of that but he is sure there is alcohol in there from the name of it. He'll go straight, as usual.

"Excuse me, bar-tender?" he calls out. "I'll have a Lemon Drop Martini and a straight Johnny Walker please."

Within a minute, the two drinks are sitting in front of them. John takes a sip of his while Lina digs into her purse. She turns to John and smiles. He can feel himself melting into the bar stool.

She suddenly gets up and steps away from the bar. She starts heading towards the bathroom. "I be back soon..." she says, turning her head towards him whilst her hips sway from side to side. He now notices that she is wearing a body hugging black dress that runs down the length of her thighs and leaves little to the imagination. She has the most beautiful pear-shaped bottom and John feels the heat building around his collar and a stir makes itself known around his groins. He hopes she didn't notice his eyes lingering a bit too long at her shapely ass...or maybe it would be good if she did.

He needs to find out more about her. Why doesn't she want to go home? It's not that John cares, it might actually be a good sign for him.

By the time she comes back, he has already finished half his whiskey. He is feeling more courageous now. She settles next to him. He nostrils flair as he inhales her scent - she's put on some perfume. Her lips are also redder now and he notices that her small scar is almost invisible.

"Wow..." he whispers, finding it hard to breathe. "You look...amazing..."

Lina blushed a little and looks at her hands. "Thank you John. Not often someone tell me this."

"Seriously? Lina you're a very beautiful woman. Doesn't your husband give you compliments?" He knows he shouldn't be asking, but he needs to find out more.

She looks up. The smile fades from her face. John can see sadness in her eyes.

"No, my husband no give me compliment. At beginning things very good. And then he not nice to me. He very jealous."

"Oh," says John. "I'm so sorry to hear that..."

Lina takes a sip of her drink. She looks at John with a

wavering smile. "No, is OK. I use to it now."

"What? Used to him not being nice to you?"

"Yes," she hesitates. "Also used him beat me when drink much vodka."

John is taken aback. "Wha...what?" Her husband beats her? What kind of man beats a woman? John has heard, of course, that some women get beaten by their husband, but to meet a girl who actually does get beaten is a whole different thing.

"Did you call the police? Or a help line maybe? I mean there are people out there who can help you, you know?"

" No. Maybe is my fault. Maybe I not good wife and make him angry. I his wife and must listen him..."

John picks up his drink and sculls it in one shot. He makes a grimace as the whiskey hits the pit of his stomach.

"No Lina! No, that's not right! No one should beat a woman, no matter what. There's no excuse for doing such a thing."

He is surprised to hear the anger in his voice. Lina's shrinks back. There is fear in her eyes, like a caged animal. John realizes he has scared her.

"Oh no," he apologizes. "I'm sorry Lina. I didn't mean to raise my voice. I'm sorry, I just got angry when you told me that your husband beats you...please forgive me..."

Lina gives him a glance and picks up her glass.

"Can I buy you drink?" she asks, the smile returning to her face.

"Oh errrr...sure." mumbles John, still feeling guilty for raising his voice.

Lina looks around and eyes the bar tender.

"One Johnny Walker straight and one Lemon Drop Martini please."

John is not used to women buying him drinks. He pulls out his wallet to pay but as he takes out a twenty, he feels her hand on his.

"No, I buy you drink John. You are nice man. Is my pleasure."

John nods. No words come out of his mouth. All his senses are focused on her hand on his. She is not moving it away and he doesn't want her to. The twenty-dollar bill is still sitting in his hand but he doesn't want to put it back in his wallet, not just yet. He doesn't want to remove his hand from under hers.

Her hand is small. Her fingers are long and thin and the bright red nail polish is a contrast with her milky white skin. Can you fall in love with a hand? He is starting to wonder.

He looks up at her. He realizes that the whiskey is sitting in front of him and she is already sipping on her Martini. He was so lost in the moment that he didn't even see the drinks coming.

Lina is smiling at him. She slowly pulls her hand away, pulls out a twenty and hands it over to the bar-tender.

"Keep change please" she says.

"Thank you mam." replies the bar-tender.

John leaves his hand on the counter for a few seconds more, hoping that hers will return. It doesn't and he reluctantly puts the twenty back into his wallet. What does he think? That it's going to be that easy?

After an awkward silent he finally says "Thanks for the drink. It's nice of you Lina."

She looks at him and moves closer.

"You welcome John. I happy you come and talk with me. Is nice to talk. Always is just me and husband. Always same people, same friends. Thank you John..."

John cannot move. He is hypnotized by her eyes. It's like they are looking straight into his soul, possessing him, making him feel aware of all his senses at once. He could get lost in those eyes.

"Oh the pleasure is all mine. And it's also nice to meet you. You are a very beautiful woman Lina and I'm happy that we met."

She smiled at him. He thinks about her husband hitting her. He feels angry inside. She is really beautiful and he cannot understand why anyone would want to hurt her.

John wonders what it would be like to hold her in his arms, to kiss her, to make love to her...

"What you thinking John? " she breaks his thoughts - again he was totally lost.

"Oh errr...nothing special" he mumbles.

She smiles. "Really?"

He suddenly feels that she can read his mind. Is it so obvious on his face how much he would love to take her home?

"Well..honestly? No. I was thinking of you..."

She leans closer. He can smell her perfume. She smells like wild flowers. He slowly inhales through his nostrils to take in more of her scent. He can feel himself stiffening and all his senses seem to come alive. He can almost hear her breath, her heartbeat, the power of her seduction.

"Oh yes?" she whispers. "And what you thinking John?"

"Well, you know, I mean...you and me?" His eyebrows arch questionably. Might as well get straight to the point.

She slowly takes a sip from her drink. John's eyes are drawn to her lips. The way she is sucking at her straw. Her neck. Her Adam's apple slowly moving up and down as she swallows. He is afraid that the stir in his pants might start to be noticeable and shift his weight uncomfortably.

The air conditioning is humming but he feels the heat rising from within, like a volcano ready to erupt.

Her own eyebrows now rise up. "You and me?" she asks innocently.

Maybe he got the wrong vibes? He takes a nervous sip, giving him a few seconds to cool down.

"Well, you know...I mean...I like you, and..." he takes up his courage - screw the school-kid attitude. "Should we go back to my place and have another drink there?"

Lina looks at him sideways, her lips still closed around the straw. Then they part and open only slightly, the bright red lipstick making them stick together for just a second. She smiles. "Yes John...I think is nice.."

***

He doesn't even make it to the kitchen where the small stash of booze is kept. He thinks that maybe they could have a couple of drinks first before hitting the sack, but as soon as they enter his tiny apartment and he shuts the door behind him, her lips are on his.

She tastes like vodka and he can feel her body pressed against his. Before he knows it, she is leaning on him, using all her strength to push him to the couch – her lips never parting with his.

As soon as his body stumbles onto the couch, she rises one leg and sits on top of him, facing him. Lina looks into his eyes and smiles. He opens his mouth to say something but she puts a finger to his lips and he feels her hips starting to sway and her pelvis pressing hard against his swelling manhood. He can feel himself getting hard and he rises his hips to meet her rhythm.

She stops kissing him for a minute, but her hips never stop their rhythm like the endless waves of an ocean.

John grabs her dress, which is now riding well above her panties. They are red - Russian red. He pulls it above her head and as soon as the dress is laying on the floor, her lips are hard pressed against his again. Her tongue hungry for his.

He feels her hands come down and in one smooth motion, his button is undone and his zip is down. She rises up in order for him to pull his pants down and his head is now at the level of her breasts. They are small yet beautiful and firm. He takes one and puts his mouth to it, sucking it hard and feeling her chest pressed against his hunger.

His erection is now standing straight like a soldier at attention and she leans back using her right hand to pull at her panties and guide him inside her. Lina sinks all the way down until he feels her buttocks against his thighs.

He closes his eyes and focuses all his attention on the tight warm envelopment of her swollen canal. She starts to riding him...all the way in...and all the say out. He feels the full length of his shaft swallowed by her unceasing desire.

Her rhythm increases and the slow tidal waves he was riding a few minutes ago have now risen to swells that are threatening to drown him in his own ecstasy. He can feel his member being swallowed and the tightness surrounding it is becoming more and more slippery as each wave meets the shore at the base of his engorged shaft.

The world stops to exist. There is only her now. He holds her tight and feels her quivering body against his. Her thighs press against his outer buttocks in an effort to stop the uncontrollable shacking.

He knows that this is the moment. He pushes her down hard. He wants to go as deep as he can. He wants her to feel all of him. Her spasms become more intense. He feels the heat rising below – like a volcano ready to erupt. He cannot hold it anymore and explodes inside her as she leans all the way back, her legs shaking., her toes curling.

He can only hear their panting now. Their bodies exhausted in the heat of their passion.

8

They stay like this for a few minutes, like two ragged dolls carelessly thrown on the couch, too worn-out to move. John can feel his heart starting to slow down. His eyes are still closed but he feels her heartbeat against his chest. Thump thump...thump thump...the beat of love.

He rises his hand and lays it at the back of her head which is nestled at where his neck and shoulder meet. He can feel her breath against his neck, like a soft summer breeze. He inhales and his nostrils are filled with a scent of musk and the floral perfume still lingering on her skin.

Lina moans, kisses his neck and her lips move up to meet his again. They are warm and moist. Her tongue finds his and slowly starts to move, teasing him again, little by little. He is not sure if he has anything left in him until he feels a stir in his loins.

John hands go down to her buttocks. He grabs each cheek. They feel warm and firm against his palms. His powerful thighs lifts her up easily. He is glad that those hours at the gym finally come to some use.

Lina buries her head in his neck and he slowly takes her to the bedroom. His bed is still unmade from this morning but he doesn't think she will mind He deposits her gently onto the crumbled sheets, her shaped reminding him of gentle hills covering a vista of snow, her skin matching the whiteness of the sheets.

Lina is just lying there, not moving. Her body unresistant to his tongue which is now slowly moving from her neck down to her navel until it finally reaches the gentle mound that defines his desires.

His hands slowly opens her legs, revealing the petals within. Again Lina doesn't resist. His eager tongue finds its way into the depths of her opened flower. He closes his eyes. He can taste her.

Her hips start to gently move up and down. He pushes his tongue deeper into her and feels her fingers at the back of his head, driving him on.

His senses are filled with the taste and smell of her previous discharge. His mouth is hungry for her. He has never been so hungry for a woman. His hands find her buttocks again, lifting her eagerness to his face. He moves his tongue deep inside her and hears her scream. Her legs open wider as she thrusts her hips to meet his hunger.

9

"Take me John..." she gasps between panting breaths with her Russian accent. "Take me again. I want feel you inside me...deep inside me..."

His head finally comes up for air. He looks down at her. Her legs are opened wide. Waiting for him. Her body swaying, inviting him to enter her again.

This time he wants to take it slowl. He wants to enjoy every sensations and remember every moment. He enters her, gently, their rhythm in unison as if they had done this a hundred times before.

Lina opens her eyes as their love making continues. She is looking deep into his own eyes and John feels his heart tighten. It doesn't just feel like sex with a stranger anymore, it's much more than that...could he be falling in love?

He moves on top of her. He wants to feel her whole body underneath his. Lina wraps her legs around him, pushing him in. He has never felt like this before, all his previous relationships seem dull next to this. He feels an intimacy he has never known. He squeezes tighter. She responds by wrapping her arms around him, her nails digging into his back.

Their momentum starts to increase. The passion mounting with each stroke. John can hear her heavy breathing and being turned on, he can now hear his own moaning starting to rise. Her hands reach down to his buttocks and push him up, deeper into her.

"Deeper my love..." she moans as her hips rise up to meet his.

My love. She has called him her love. He can feel the passion burning him up. He pushes harder, every nerve in his body responding to her needs. He wants to give it all to her. He never wants to let her go. He puts his hand behind her head and cuddles it into his shoulder.

Lina lets out a sob. He doesn't know if it's from sadness or happiness, pain or pleasure. He feels a sharp pain in his shoulder as her teeth sink into the soft flesh at the base of his neck. But he loves it - the ecstasy, the pain, the pleasure.

Their rhythm increases and what was love making now becomes and irrational tangle of limbs. Their mouths, hungry for flesh, seeking any place that they can find — to bite, to taste.. to drink up the sweat that is now drenching their bodies.

He can feel the heat rising, every pore of his body letting out a steam of passion, every nerve that she touches burning like the fire of their intensity. He feels her body convulsing underneath him and the spasms that accompany the almost inhuman cry that escapes from her mouth as she reaches orgasm again and again.

He cannot hold it any longer. It would be like trying to stop a speeding bullet from entering his chest. He explodes, his body shaking uncontrollably, like the leaves of a tree in a hurricane of sensations.

Their bodies are now lying on the floor in a heap of tangled sheets, her head resting on his chest, their breathing slowing down and their beating hearts welcoming the interlude of their mad gallop. Together they lay. Their minds escaping from the harsh realities of life. It is only them now, in their own cocooned shelter of love, passion and desire.

***

John hears water running. His mind is confused. His eyes flutter open. It's still dark. What's he doing on the floor?

Then it hits him. Something is amiss...Lina?

He hears the bathroom door open and the sudden light streaming from it makes him shut his eyes tight.

He tries to get up but his body only responds with aches and pains. It obviously doesn't like spending the night on the hard floor and it makes sure that John knows it.

He looks at the alarm clock beside his bed - 3 A.M.

"Lina?" he manages through a series of grants. "Why are you up?"

"Sssshhhhh my dear..." she replies, stepping out of the bathroom. "I must to go John."

"But...it's 3 A.M." he mumbles, trying to get his eyes to open and his numb body to respond.

Lina wriggles into her tight dress and John ,finally opening an eye, feels a stir. "Is late and my husband already send text. I tell him birthday party finish and now come home. He sound not happy..."

John rubs his eyes. "Oh...errrrr...will you be OK? Do you want to me come with you? I can just make sure you get home OK."

Lina picks up her shoes, giving John a good view of her

booty. He manages to get on the bed and seats at the edge. He looks down at his increasing growth and, a little embarrassed, picks up the sheet to cover it.

"No, is OK John, no worry about me. I'm OK. My home not so far. I need get home now. Husband will angry..."

He can see fear written all over her face, the panicked way in which she rushes to buckle up her shoes., her hands shaking.

He gets up and doesn't notice the sheet falling on the floor. He walks over to her and takes her hand in his. "Hey...are you sure you're OK? You seem...scared."

Lina looks up at him. She forces a strained smile. Her lips trembled. "John, I not know. When husband angry, sometime he loose control."

John puts his arms around her. She looks like a lamb that knows its heading for the slaughter house. He wants to hold her and protect her. Why does he feel this way? It's not like it's the first time he's picked up a girl for a one night stand. But there is something different about her. Is there such a thing as love at first sight? John thought this was a myth, but now he is starting to wonder. He brings her closer into his arms. He wants to hold her and never let her go.

"Listen...it's going to be OK" he says, not really believing it. "Why don't you stay? Maybe you can tell him you're a bit drunk and prefer to stay at your friend's place..."

Lina takes half a step back, her small hands pushing at his chest, creating a void between them. "I can't, I must to go home. Husband angry, if stay longer, more angry."

"Lina. I'm worried about you. Will he hurt you? You said he has hit you before..."

Her hands drop to her side. Her lips tighten. "I not know...please John, I must to go now...."

John takes her head between his hands and puts his lips to hers. This time she doesn't resist. Her mouth opens and he can taste his own toothpaste. He closes his eyes. He wants to remember her. He wants to remember this moment – the way she feels, the way she tastes.

Her body starts to sinks into his. John can feel her thighs against his, the warmth of her body, the tongue that is slowly caressing his. His body responds. He can feel his manhood pressing against her - responding to her touch.

Suddenly, her head jerks away and her lips part with his. "We can't do this...I go now...please John, let go me..."

She takes a step back and her body slides away from his until only one finger remains between his thumb and index. He doesn't want to let her go. He doesn't want to loose her.

"Please," he begs. "Can I at least have your number? I want to see you again..I *have* to see you again."

She pulls her hand away, leaving an emptiness at the pit of his stomach. She reaches into her handbag and takes out a pen and a small notepad. She scribbles something.

"Not call me OK? Just text. You nice man John. I can feel. I also want see you again." She hands him the note.

John takes it and doesn't look at it. He just wants to look at her face. He just wants to remember. He tries to take her hand again but Lina turns and heads towards the door.

"Lina..." he pleads one last time.

She opens the front door and turns to him, a sad smile crossing her face. "My sweet John..." she whispers.

And then...she's gone.

CHAPTER 2

John is sitting at his desk – but his mind is somewhere else. Lina...

After she had left, he hadn't been able to go back to sleep. He kept worrying about her and if she was going to be OK once she got home. At 7 A.M the alarm had gone off and with sleepy eyes, he had managed to get to the bathroom. Her scent had still been still lingering, making it hard for him to get her out of his mind.

Now sitting here, all he can think of is her. She seems to be filling every corner of his mind. He remembers their love making - every details running through his head. Her smell, her touch, her white skin against the white sheets, and the way she moaned as the intensity of their sexual encounter enveloped them in frantic, uncontrollable spasms of desires.

He doesn't remember feeling this way for anyone before. This wasn't just sex. It was more than that. Love? Again, he begins to wonder. Was it meant to be? Was he supposed to meet her in that bar? Was it more than just a one-night stand?

John tries to focus on the screen in front of him. He can't. Maybe he should have just stayed at home - this is useless. There is no way he will get anything done today, not with Lina covering his every thought, like fresh snow, making everything blank.

He needs a coffee. He needs to talk to James.

He knows James will listen to him and understand him. They have been best friends for almost eight years now and have shared just about everything, and *this* is definitely something he wants to – no, needs to – share with him. He dials James' number.

***

James hands him a steaming hot Americano. John takes a sip and feels his taste buds welcoming the strong, black caffeine – he needed that.

"Sooooo...what's up dude? Kind of early for morning tea, ain't it?" James says, sitting himself down on the black plastic canteen chair.

John pulls up a chair and sits himself down. He swears to himself that these chairs are meant to be as uncomfortable as possible to make sure that you don't spend your whole morning in the canteen sipping coffee.

He takes another sip – at least the coffee's good.

"Well...where should I start." he mumbles.

"Beginning would be good." says James. "What mischiefs have you been up to this time dude?"

John smiles. He friend always has a knack for knowing that something's going on. Mischief? Guess you could call it that. "I met this girl." he replies.

"Met this girl..." James smirks. "Well?...So?"

"Well. It's complicated. It was suppose to be just a one-night stand, but somehow it feels...more than that."

"OK.....how's that? You're not falling in love with a girl yous just screwed once, are you?"

"Mmmmm...I think I might be." says John, not looking up, his mind filled with her face. "You wouldn't understand though buddy...I mean, she really is something special."

He looks up and sees James slowly put his coffee down, his eyes not leaving him. His eyes narrow and one corner of his mouth comes up. "Tell me. And don't leave anything out..."

"Her name's Lina..."

"Lina? That doesn't sound very English. Is that Russian?"

"Yep, she is Russian. Well anyway. Met her last night and -"

James' brows shoot up. "Wow...wow...wait a minute! Last night? In love? So fast?"

"Wait buddy. Let me explain, then maybe you'll understand."

"OK...OK..sorry. Tell me."

"Right," continues John, taking another sip. "I met her at LKF. I was just bored and needed a drink. Next thing you know, I was looking up and there she was. Buddy, she was like...wow! The kind of girl you wouldn't get near coz you know you wouldn't stand a chance."

"Mmmmhhhhh..." mumbles James, leaning forward.

"So...anyway. After mastering up all my courage and another few sips of whiskey, I finally got the guts to head over and talk to her. I thought she would probably tell me she was waiting for her husband or tell me to piss off."

"And she did right?" laughed James.

John smiles "No, as a matter of fact she didn't. And actually she was even more beautiful from close up. She has these short blonde hair, incredible gray-green eyes and an amazing white skin. Dude...I mean she looks like a model!"

James takes a sip of his coffee, grimaces and puts it down. John knows that James hates his coffee getting warm. He likes it extra hot or nothing. He once mentioned he enjoys drinking hot coffee, not warm cat piss. "So what dude? You're saying you're in love with a girl you met once in a bar?"

"*And* spent the night with.." retorts John defensively.

"Oh yes...*and* spent the night with her," says James with sarcasm in his voice. "Dude, it's obvious you're infatuated. She is the hottest girl your little pecker has probably ever met after what probably adds up to her having had one too many, *and* you are confusing this with love."

"No, seriously. It's not only that. Although I have to admit the sex was amazing...it's not just her looks buddy. It's...I don't know. Do...do you believe in love at first sight?"

The smile fades from James' lips and a deep furrow appears between his eyebrows. "Wow...you're serious aren't you? You really are falling in love with this girl..."

John takes one last sip of his now almost cold brew. "Yep. I really think I'm. I don't understand why, but there's something about her." He looks at his watch. "Oh crap, need to go buddy, having a conference call in five minutes. Mmmmmm...wish me luck. I have no idea how I'll be able to concentrate."

***

John hangs up the phone. The conference call went well, although most of the time he was barely listening – lost in his own thoughts. All he could see was her beautiful face and the thin scar that runs down from her lip. Did her husband do that to her?

He feels anger building up inside. He wants to protect her. No woman deserves to be hit. Only cowards and weak assholes hit women. He'd love to beat the shit of him in a dark alley. "See how you'd feel, you low-life scum..." he mumbles to himself, his teeth and fists clenched.

He shakes his head. He has to stop thinking about her. He has a lot of work to do. He opens the online document, trying to get his thoughts back in the game.

***

John checks his watch again – 10 A.M. He feels he's been doing this a thousand times today. Why hasn't she called him yet? - Or at least send him a message. Did last night mean as much to her as it did to him? Is he just imaging that the look in her eyes meant nothing? Was *he* just a one-night stand to her?

Or maybe something happened to her? Her husband? An accident?

John takes his cell phone out again. He pulls the piece of paper out of his pocket and decides to take the risk and send her a message. He hesitates for a second and then his fingers start typing.

- *Hi, this is John. Could you please call me back on this number? Something urgent. Thanks.*

OK. not the most romantic of a message after spending a night together but he doesn't want to take a chance in case her husband happens to check her phone.

John waits for a while and – nothing. This is no good, and he can't call her – too risky. He decides to put his head down and start focusing on this work. Worrying is not going to

17

change anything and his work is not going to get done by itself.

The document in front of him looks blurry. He can feel the onset of a headache. He closes his eyes tightly for a minute and after reopening them, the document has lost some of its blurriness. OK...back to work.

His fingers start typing. The letters that appear on the screen are automatic. Half of his brain isn't present – it's still haunted by Lina. He shakes his head. Come on!...snap out of it John! Worrying isn't going to make any difference. She is probably OK and having a game of tennis with her friends now...

Bzzzzzz...Bzzzzzz

John quickly picks up his cell. *LINA*...it says, a message. His heart leaps and skips a beat. He quickly enters the password.

- H

That's all...just a H. what's that suppose to mean? His fingers move faster than he can think.

- H? Lina? Is that you?

He waits, his eyes fixated on the message - not daring to move. He can feel his heart beating like a drum against this chest. A bead of sweat forms high up on his brow and slowly makes its way down his face. He wipes it off unconsciously.

- Lina? Are you OK? his moist fingers automatically type.

Bzzzzzz....

*- **HELP***

He feels the hairs on his arms stand. A cold sweat covers him. What's happening? Why would she ask for help? Screw the risk. He quickly dials her number.

Brrrrrr...Brr...Brrrrr...Brr...Brrrrrr...Brr...Brrrr...Brr...Brrrrrr Brr...Brrrrr...Brr...

Nothing. No reply. He hangs up and starts typing as fast as his fingers will allow on the tiny cell keyboard.

- U OK? What's wrong? Send me address. I come over...

He can smell himself. A primal smell of fear. - acidic and foul. He hates his own smell. He hates himself for not being able to help. She needs him and he can only seat here and do nothing.

He redials. Nothing - no ringing. And then, an unfamiliar robotic female voice.

- The number you have called is currently not available. Please try again later...

He quickly redials...his hand shacking.

- The number you ha...

He hangs up. His head is swimming with a sudden dizziness. He feels his body falling back and barely catches the edge of his desk. He pulls himself back up. Bile rises to his throat. He can taste the bitterness. He feels he going to be sick - the fear in him wanting to escape. His mind is racing. He can only see her face now - her pleading eyes, and there is nothing he can do...

CHAPTER 3

John doesn't know what to do and what to think. He tries to calm himself down but his eyes keep going back to his cell.

He picks up his office phone and quick-dials James' extension.

"Buddy. I need to talk to you..."

"Yep, what's up dude?" James asks.

"I mean like face to face. I need to talk to you now...face to face."

"Are you OK dude? You don't sound so good"

"No, I'm not. Meet me at the pantry OK? My treat..." He hangs up.

***

John brings the steaming hot coffee to his lips and takes a sip. He closes his eyes for a minute, trying to reorganize his thoughts.

"So?"

He opens his eyes. James is looking at him, a concerned look on his face.

"Sorry" John apologizes. "I just can't believe this is happening...."

James raises his eyes in impatience. "Happening? What? Are you gonna spit it out or leave me hanging there? I have work to do...deadlines, you know?"

"Sorry..sorry. OK, well, you know the girl I was telling you about earlier on?"

"Lina? The Russian girl?" James asks, bringing the brew to his lips.

"Yes, her. Well, I didn't hear from her and..."

"Well what did you expect dude? It was a one-night stand..."

"No. No, please it's not that, let me finish." John says.

"OK, I'm sorry, continue."

John takes another sip "OK." he sighs. "After last night I didn't hear anything from her and I wanted to make sure she was OK. I was worried about her."

James frowns. "Worried? Why? I'm sure she got home OK dude."

"That's the thing though. I'm also sure she got home OK. But, there's more..."

"What do you mean more?" asks James, wiping is mouth with the back of his hand.

"She is married," replies John "And...she told me that when her husband gets angry, he beats her."

James's eyes open wide and he leans forward on his elbows. "Wh...what?" he exclaims. "Married? And...he what?"

John looks around and back at James. "Keep it down buddy...we don't have to let the whole world to know."

James blushes. "Sorry, sorry..." he apologizes leaning closer. "Married OK. Happens. But what do you mean, he beats her?" he whispers. "Like really beat her? You know, like abuse?"

John shakes his head in disbelief. "Who cares how? He beats her and that's it, and that's wrong. Simple!"

"OK...OK! Don't get your nickers in a knot. So you were worried. I understand. Right, so you called her?"

"No. I didn't want to call her in case her husband picked up the phone. So I sent her a text."

James' furrow deepens. "Mmmmmh...and, did she reply?" he asks.

John sighs and shakes his head. "No. Well not right away anyway."

"So, she did reply then."

"Yes. Eventually. But only one word..."

James leans forward, a questioning and impatient look crossing his face.

"Help..." John says.

"Help?" asks James confused.

John hands are shaking. He puts his cup down. "Yes. That was the word. Just.. help." he says.

"Shit dude!" James says too loud. "Sorry..." he lowers his voice. "I mean. *Shit* dude. What do you think happened? Help? Just help? Nothing else?"

John looks down for a second, trying to make sense of it all. Trying to see if he has missed anything. He checks his cell again. Nothing. "Wait." he says.

He dials Lina's number and puts the phone to his ear.

- The number you...

He hangs up and slams the cell down on the table, not caring anymore if anyone sees him. "Shit. Still can't get through. Disconnected."

"It doesn't ring?" James asks.

"No. After her message, I tried to call her several times but looks like her cell has been switched off. It keeps saying the number is not available right now. Man, what do I do? Should I call the police?"

James frowns. "OK...OK. Let's not get into high gear yet. I mean, maybe they just had an argument and...that's it."

"Well, yea...maybe. But what about the help message? Doesn't that show that something is *really* wrong? I mean, I wouldn't send a help message unless it was bad right?"

James shakes his head. "Dude, this may look worse than what it is... maybe it's just a lover's spat. I think maybe you should give it a day or two, and in the meantime you can try calling her back. You know, maybe her phone just ran out of battery. And, if she really needed desperate help, don't you think she would have called the cops before texting you? Maybe she doesn't want the cops involved. I mean, you know., you don't want to drag the cops in every-time you have a marital dispute."

John knows his friend is right but his guts tell him otherwise. "I don't know buddy. I have a bad feeling about this. Something is definitely wrong. I can feel it. I'm not sure, maybe you're right, maybe I should wait a day...or two."

James looks at his watch and gets up. He rests his hand on John's shoulder. "Yes. I think that'd be best dude. I mean you don't want to get her in trouble with her husband in case it's really nothing." He looks at his watch again and his mouth twitches. "I really need to go. Have a meeting in an hour and a lot to prepare...sorry..."

John looks at his own watch, takes a last swallow of his now-cold-coffee and puts it down with a grimace. "Yea, I also need to get back. I have a lot to do but I just can't focus." He shakes his head and looks down – his eyes unfocused. "Buddy....I'm really worried and I hope you're right. I hope she is OK..."

CHAPTER 4

John takes the keys out of his pants pocket. His hands are shaking. He still has a lot of work sitting on his desk but he's decided that he wouldn't be able to get through it; not today anyway - not with Lina invading his mind.

He opens the front door and switches the light on then decides he'd rather be in shadows. The sun is making its descent, just touching the horizon, but there is enough light filtering in from the street light outside his apartment. He switches it off, he needs to think.

He takes the three steps leading to the small bar at the corner of the lounge room and pulls out a half empty bottle of Jack Daniels. He prefers Scotch but hasn't had the chance to replace his empty bottle of Ballantine. Losers can't be choosers.

He thinks of going into the kitchen to add his usual three ice-cubes but straight sounds like what he really needs right now. He fills the glass to one third, hesitates for a second and adds another couple of nips for good measure.

With his glass now half full, he takes the two steps that lead him to his favorite Starbucks-style armchair – big, well-worn and comfy.

Lina...he shakes his head. No. He has to stop thinking of

her before he drives himself crazy. It's no use. All he can do is wait and hope and pray. Not much of a believer but hey...desperate times need desperate measures; and if anyone knows what's going on, it would be HIM.

"Please GOD," he whispers. "If you really are out-there...I beg of you. Let my Lina be OK."

John chuckles. "My Lina?" he mumbles to himself. "Oh, she is your Lina now, is she?" The corner of his lip rises into a lop-sided smile he really doesn't feel.

An image of her sitting on him – riding him, appears in his mind, and then, it is replaced with her lips. The thin scar. Her beautiful face. That bastard. How could a husband do this? How could he hit her to the point of cutting her lip. He imagines the fist – *his* fist. Her lip splitting open like an overripe fruit hitting the ground. The shocked look in her eyes – the fear. The next fist that rattles every bone in her head.

He doesn't want to think. He brings the whiskey to his lips and feels the smooth amber liquid descend to the pit of his stomach. The whiskey has the desired effect. He can feel his body relax – every muscle loosing its tension and his anger slowly dissipating like a river flowing down a gentle hill.

He closes his eyes and leans his head all the way back, draining the remaining liquor and expecting the usual sensation of the ice-cubes bumping against his teeth. But they don't. He remembers - screw the ice.

He looks at the empty glass, sighs and leans forward, trying to get the bulk of his weight onto his feet. He manages to retain his balance – barely.

Two steps later, his glass is being refilled, with shaky hands, but this time, the whiskey reaches the rim before the bottle finds its way upright again. He looks at the glass, puts it down and heads back to the armchair – bottle in hand.

He takes a swig while his other hand digs into his pocket for the cell. He presses the redial button and waits for the robotic voice, and as sure as he is sitting here with his bottle in hand, the sound of hopelessness reaches his ear.

- *The numb...*

His thumb pressed the red button and he lets the cell slip from his hand. He hears the muffled sound as it hits the carpet.

The bottle reaches his lips. He can feels his Adam's apple

moving up and down as the liquid makes its way down fast, polluting his blood and clouding his mind.

His eyes are heavy and the weight of his body is pulling him down. He can feel himself sinking into the leather seat. Numbness starts to take hold, rending his muscles into a useless puppet-like heaviness. The heavy lids that mask his eyes shut the last sliver of light that attempts to penetrate his pupils.

The bottle slowly leaves his opened fingers, landing horizontally and spilling the remaining booze onto the white carpet which sucks up the violating whiskey, leaving a light brown offending discoloration.

***

He is sitting at the bar – his whiskey in hand. He looks up. She is there – Lina. *His* Lina.

He knows her, he knows he does. He feels it within his guts - a strong sense of dejà-vu. How does he even know her name? Has he met her before? No way, he would definitely remember meeting someone as beautiful as that.

John picks up his whiskey and without looking at what's left inside the glass, he brings it to his lips and downs the remaining one and a half shots. He feels the alcohol make its way down to the pit of his stomach and instantly, the butterflies he was feeling within vanish and are replaced with a lightheartedness that give him the courage to leave the protection of the bar and make his way to her – to his Lina. How the hell does he know her name? He is sure that he has never met her before.

Lina turns to meet his eyes - almost as if she knew he was coming. Her mouth opens and time suddenly seems to slow down as her lips begin to form a word.

John is wavering towards her, the whiskey making its effect felt. He feels more like he is floating. He suddenly notices that slowly, her body is beginning to vanish. He shuts his eyes tight and re-opens them.

He can now see the bar-tender walking behind her, expect something doesn't seem right. The bar-tender is indeed behind her but he can still see *all* of him, as if she wasn't there – as if she were starting to vanish.

He tries to hasten his pace. He feels he needs to get to her before she is totally gone. Her mouth continues to open and his eyes focus on her lips – her almost transparent lips.

A word is forming. John can read it easily, can almost hear it – HELP. He looks into her eyes and sees pure horror and fear in them. He tries to run faster now, but he can't. Everything seems to be happening in slow motion.

John is almost there. He reaches out to touch her, but before he does, her body vanishes and all that is left behind is her drink sitting on the bar. His hand passes through the void that replaces the space she was occupying just a second ago, but comes into contact with nothing but thin air.

"Lina...no!!!" he hears his own mind screaming.

And then his eyes open...

CHAPTER 5

"It was only a dream dude. I mean come on... you don't believe in dreams do you?"

John looks out the window of the staff canteen. After having woken up from his dream, he hadn't been able to go back to sleep. He had ended up tossing and turning and in the end, had come in to work at the ungodly hour of 5 A.M.

At least he did manage to get some work done, even-though the image of Lina at the bar had been haunting every corner of his mind.

Now seating here with a warm coffee in hand and the onset of a headache due to lack of sleep *and* an overdose of whiskey, he takes a sip and leans towards James.

"I'm telling your buddy, *this* is not an ordinary dream. It was like...she...Lina, was trying to talk to me."

James shakes his head in disbelief. "Mate, there is no such thing as people communicating through dreams. Gees...come on, wake up!"

John puts his cup down. He knows he must sounds like an imbecile but it felt so real...well except for the part when she disappeared that is.

"And I'm telling *you*....it was almost like she was trying to communicate with me." He pauses and frowns. "Like she was trying to tell me something. *Help*...just like the message."

James' mouth twists to one side and he looks up at the

ceiling. "Right, just like the message, which means exactly that; a dream from what happened yesterday. It isn't like she said anything else now is it?"

"Well, she didn't have the chance since she disappeared anyway." John replies defensively.

James takes a sip of his coffee. "OK, OK" he said raising his hands in surrender. "It's too early to argue, so fine, have it your way. And so now what anyway?"

John sighs. "I don't know," he says. He puts his head between his hands and closed his eyes. "I really don't know. Do you think it's time to call the police?"

"No. Give it another day. Like I said, probably just an argument and you don't want to get the police involved for a stupid domestic dispute. I'm sure the cops have some real criminals to catch mate."

"OK, then what? I mean...I can't just do nothing can I? I need to know what happened to her and why she's not calling me back."

James thinks for a moment, rubbing the stubble on his chin. "Mmmmmm...let's say her cell's broken OK? Then, that would explain why she can't call you back coz she doesn't have your number now, does she?'

"OK, and..." John says impatiently.

"Annnnd...why don't you go back to the bar tonight and see if she is around? Maybe she'll go back there hoping to see you also. Especially since you are telling me it's true love..." James smiles.

"Funny..." John says unamused. "But maybe you're right. Maybe I'm making a big deal out of nothing. It probably is just an argument and nothing else."

James gets up. "Time to go dude. Just go there after work and see what happens OK?"

"OK buddy. Will do, and...thanks for being there..."

James smiles and looks at his watch. "Anytime dude...let's go."

***

It's only 6 P.M. and the bar is almost empty. John looks around quickly and counts only five people, including the bar-

29

tender, but Lina isn't one of them.

He feels disappointed. He can almost see her in his mind's eye, sitting there, sipping on a vodka. Then her eyes would meet his. Her smile would follow and then he would know that everything's OK. Even in his car, on the way to the bar, he was preparing what he would say to her and they would laugh at the fact that he was thinking of calling the cops.

But this is not the case.

The real scenario is that she is not here. John looks at his watch again, 6:03 P.M. Maybe it's too early? What did he expect? That she would seat at bar all day waiting for him to show up? That she was going to come back for him? They only had met one night and in the end, no matter how he felt about her, she might have been on a totally different page. Maybe he had just been a number – another pick-up for her to escape her bad marriage.

He walks to the bar and orders a double Johnny Walker straight. He could be here for a while. He looks around again. Perhaps he's missed her.

Nothing.

Maybe she is, right now, in another bar, getting picked up by some other moron. Or maybe she is lying in someone else's arms. The thought of someone else holding her makes him jealous to the core. He hates feeling this way.

He looks at his drink and the idea of sculling it comes to mind, but then he decides against it. What if she shows up? He wants to make sure that he is sober and doesn't make a dick out of himself. After all, they had only met once. So, was it just about sex for her? Animal instinct? No, John refuses to believe that. He knows it had been more than that – more than a one night stand. The way she had looked into his eyes - into his soul. The way they had held each-other tight and how she had held his hand before landing a gentle, moist kiss on his lips.

He closes his eyes and touches his lips – remembering. And the last words she had said to him before leaving. *My sweet John...*

This had to mean something. John doesn't want to believe that this was the end. He has to see her again. He *needs* to see her again.

He hears the entrance door of the bar behind him. Steps. Heels.

His heart skips a beat. He can already feels her lips against his ear. Her moist lips whispering *Hi John...*

He turns around to meet her eyes. A premature smile is already forming on his lips to let her know how happy he is to see her.

She is wearing a black coat. He looks up at her face. Her hair are dark. She is not looking at him. His heart sinks. It's not her...

The dark-haired girl walks to the table next to the counter and is greeted by a tall handsome man. They smile at each-other and she gently lays a kiss on his lips. They sit down, his hand never leaving hers.

John turns his head. He cannot bear seeing this. He closes his eyes and takes another sip of his whiskey.

***

Is it his fourth or his fifth? So much for staying sober.

He looks around again - for the hundredth time. He checks his watch - 1:04 A.M. The couple has already left an hour ago.

He feels empty. Lina... where are you Lina? Are you OK? Did he hurt you?

He looks up.

"Excuse me! Bar-tender..." he slurs.

The bar-tender walk-slides towards him with a well-practiced automated smile.

"Yes sir? Another one?" he asks.

"No thanks, I've had enough for tonight. I just have a question for you."

"Sure sir. How can I help?"

"Do you remember a couple of nights ago I was in here and there was a blonde girl sitting at the bar?"

The bar-tender frowns for a few seconds. "Yes, I think I do," he replies smiling. "And I do believe that you are the lucky gentleman who walked her out with her. Am I correct?"

John feels a sense of relief. Maybe he can help. "Yes! Yes, that was me," he says enthusiastically. "May I ask if you have seen her coming in here last night by any chance?"

The bar-tender thinks for a while. "No, I'm sorry. I don't remember seeing her last night. She definitely didn't show up."

John feels the disappointment but tries not to show it -

there is still hope. "OK," he says, pulling his wallet out and removing a business card. He passes it to the bar-tender. "If you see her tonight or any other night, could you pass her my business card and ask her to call me?"

The bar-tender takes it. "Sure sir, I can do that." he smiles. "Mmmmmm, I guess you didn't exchange phone numbers last time you met?"

"No...no, we did. It's just that...never-mind. It's complicated..."

John pulls out a fifty and hands it to the bar-tender. "Keep the change," he says. "And please make sure to give her my card. This is very important to me."

The bar-tender takes the fifty. "Yes sir. I will. She is a very beautiful lady if you don't mind me saying so and I can't blame you for wanting to see her again. I'll definitely pass on the message when...*if* I see her."

"Thanks you." John says, taking his coat from the adjacent stool. He turns around, steps down from his own stool and starts heading toward the entrance door.

His can feels his head spinning a little. He looses balance and catches himself on a table. He takes one last look around the bar – just to make sure. He is the last one to leave.

Alone...

CHAPTER 6

John opens the front door. He turns on the light and looks at the clock. Almost 2 A.M.

He heads straight for the bar. He knows he wont be able to sleep unless he sinks a couple more. He finds a half bottle of Bundaberg - forget the glass, he just grabs the bottle.

No need for lights, he thinks and switches the light off on the way to his favorite armchair.

He closes his eyes and takes his first sip, letting the rum linger in his mouth for a while, enjoying the smooth taste, before letting it go down slowly.

His mind switches to Lina. She wasn't at the bar. Well, what did he expect? Inside, he knew that she wouldn't be there, but he had to try. It's not like there were any other options open to him anyway.

Well at least the bar-tender now has his card and if she comes back she will be able to contact him. God...let it be that her phone is just broken and that's it. She probably just dropped it after sending him the message – nothing more and nothing less...hopefully.

Yes, John thinks. *That's all well and good but what about the actual message...Help?*

He shifts his weight to the corner of the armchair., trying to get more comfortable. He knows that he probably won't make it to bed tonight. He'll fall asleep right here – if he can only stop thinking.

'Help'. Why would she send that message unless she really was in trouble. That means *no*, it's not OK. Something must have happened. He imagines, again, the clenched fist landing on her lip, the one that splits it like a grape, and the ones that followed. Lina stuck in the corner of a room, not being able to move, not being able to escape the next blow. Maybe she had just been able to crawl into the bathroom and lock the door long enough to send him the distress message. Maybe she chose him because he was the last text she had received and she barely had time to press reply and type *'HELP'* before the flimsy bathroom door had flown open, splinters of wood landing at her feet. Then the final blow...

John feels himself shaking. Sadness, rage, all attacking his senses. He takes the bottle, his hand shakes uncontrollably. He brings it to his lips. The tip of the bottle rattles against his teeth. He opens his mouth wide, closes his eyes and lets the torrent of alcohol cascade down his burning throat until it runs out.

His drops the empty bottle down by the side of the armchair. It lends on its side but there is nothing left in it for the carpet to absorb.

Bastard! How could he do that! How could he hurt her! Lina! Where are you? Are you OK?

He opens his eyes. The room is spinning; everything is a blur. He feels something warm making its way down his face – a tear. He tries to raise his hand to wipe it but he has no strength left inside him. His body feels like a ragged doll – a boneless corps held together by stitches of strings. He slowly sinks into the armchair and into the abyss of his own sorrow.

He can only see her face now. Her beautiful face. And her lips, the lips he has kissed time and time again during that unforgettable night. And the scar, the thin scar that is witness to the physical abuse upon her frail body...

***

John looks up over the rim off his glass. She is there, at the other end of the bar. He doesn't know how he knows but he knows, like a premonition, that she would be. In fact, not only is she there but she was already looking at him when he looked her way; almost as if she had been expecting him.

He feels that something is going to happen. He has to hurry, else...he doesn't know why, but he knows it's important.

He gets up too quickly and stumbles. The two many whiskeys he seems to have had hit him hard. With his left hand holding on to the bar railing, he takes intoxicated steps towards her.

He bumps into someone.

"Watch it Pal!" an angry voice rings into his ear.

"Soooo....soorry buddyyyy" John manages to say as he tries to veer around the heavy set man.

He looks up. Something is wrong. Lina, *he knows her name?*, seems to be shimmering, her body becoming...translucent.

No! he knows she will be gone soon. He needs to hurry. He needs to get to her before she vanishes. He tries to takes bigger, more hurried steps, but his legs falter and feel like they are sinking into quicksand.

He is just ten feet from her now. She is looking at him, sadness filling her eyes.

Her mouth opens. She wants to say something to him, he knows it's important. He can't hear what she is saying, his ears are ringing and the bar is too loud. He feels like he's inside a bee hive and there is a million bees buzzing around him and right at the end of the hive is this tiny bee trying, in vain, to reach him.

He is almost there now...five feet. He reaches out, hoping, that maybe his touch will stop her from vanishing.

His eyed focus on her lips. She is saying something over and over again. Her lips press together, then open and form an O before opening wide. He tries to read her lips. M...I...R...A...

Then she is gone. The bar stool she was sitting on is empty – like she has never existed.

John feels his legs give in under him. He crumbles to the ground. His head hits the ground hard but he doesn't feel it; he feels only numbness and an overwhelming emptiness.

Something wet against his cheek. He barely has the strength to turn his head. He is lying in his own vomit. He looks up. All around faces are looking down at him – laughing, mocking the wasted soul drowning in his own puke.

He doesn't want to see them. He turns his head towards his own excretion and some of it enters his mouth. He doesn't care. He doesn't care about anything anymore. His mind is filled with her...

***

John's body jerks up. He looks around, the room is dark. For a moment he cannot make any sense of where he is. He sees an empty bottle of Bundaberg next to the armchair where his body is slumped like a disused piece of garbage.

He tries to move and feels every nerve screaming in response. A sharp pain, starting at his lower back, makes itself known by sending a distress signal to his brain which is starved of hydration and will eventually respond with the inevitable hangover - John, feels like shit.

He closes his eyes for a minute trying to remember how he ended up sleeping on the armchair.

He remembers the bar. Lina. He was looking for her. Hoping she would be there. He remembers the disappointment, the hollow feeling inside his guts when she didn't show up – not that he thought she would anyway.

He shakes his head. Big mistake. The impending migraine that is developing between his eyes rattles inside his head. It feels like a jack-hammer and his head is about to explode.

John manages to slowly lift his arm to his face. The pins and needles are starting to recede and a tingling sensation takes its place. He checks his watch.

5:04 A.M.

What day is it? John's not sure. *Please let it be Saturday*, he begs to himself.

He looks at his watch closer. He can hardly discern the tiny markings that make up the day and date. The room is still dark expect for the ghostly light from the street-light filtering through the lace curtains.

He squints – FRI | 6.

Damn. That means work. He needs water, lots of it. He needs to re-hydrate first then a hot shower and a strong black coffee – then maybe, just maybe, he might make it to work.

He slowly gets up. His limbs crying in agony at the torment

of a night spent on the armchair. He looks at the bottle lying on its side and bends over to pick it up. The sudden pain in his lower back tells him that it's not a good idea – later maybe...after the hot shower.

John heads straight for the kitchen sink and doesn't bother with a glass. He lets the water run for a while and brings his mouth to the faucet. He feels the icy water stream down his parched throat, awakening his senses. Once his stomach is ready to burst, he puts his whole head under the faucet and gasps as the frigid water finds a way to the base of his neck and down his back.

He jolts up and something sharp hits the back of his head – the faucet. "*Damn it!*" he curses, rubbing the small lump that is already forming on his cranium.

"OK..OK...shower," he mumbles, rubbing his head and checking his fingers for any sign of blood.

John turns on the bathroom light and the bright white neon light suddenly entering his pupils makes the jack-hammer seem like a joke.

He recoils and bends over with his palm pressed hard against his forehead, trying in vain to squeeze out the throbbing headache.

He shakes his head, slower this time, and opens a tiny slit of his left eye, just enough to find the heater switch.

He flicks it – nothing. The little red light that's suppose to show that the bathroom heater is on doesn't turn on. He tries again – still nothing.

Great...oh well. Can anything else go wrong?

He turns on the hot water. *Well, at least that works.*

John lets the water run for a while until the steam starts to fill the bathroom. He drops his clothes on the floor, not bothering with them. He just needs a nice hot shower to clear his head.

He steps into the shower and lets the hot water cascade down from the top of his head. He can already feel the warmth taking effect on his head and his lower back, his muscles relaxing as the heat penetrates.

He leans against the shower wall and lets the water run down his abused body. He closes his eyes, enjoying the sensation. Everything is slowing down. He can hear his own heartbeat drumming in his head, his headache but a dull memory now...

Mira...Mira...

He opens his eyes, coming back to reality. Mira? He remembers now. Lina, the bar, the dream! The last thing her lips had pronounced before she vanished – *Mira...*

Mira. Who is this Mira? Is it someone Lina knows? Could she help him find her?

He shakes his head. "What the...it was a dream dude..." he mutters to himself, trying to let reality set in.

Yes, it was a dream, but what if...what if it's more than that? Two days in a row now. The bar, just like their first meeting - expect for the disappearance and the messages of course. And Mira. What's that suppose to mean? If there really is a Mira, how can he possibly find her? Assuming that she exists of course.

The bathroom is filled with steam now. John can barely see his own hand in front of his face. He reluctantly turns off the hot water and steps out of the shower.

He gropes for the towel and grabs it. He can't see anything. He opens the bathroom door to let some of the steam out.

The vapor slowly dissipates out of the opened door, leaving behind a trail of ghostly smoke.

John dries his body and bring the towel to his face whilst blindly taking the two steps separating him from the sink. He leaves the towel around his shoulders and absently grabs his toothbrush. He applies a finger tip of toothpaste and extends his hand to wipe the steam off the mirror facing him.

Then he sees it....

His toothbrush falls into the sink – he doesn't even notice it. He can feel every hair on his body stand erect. His mind cannot grasp what he is seeing. His head is swimming and his heart is pounding so hard in his chest, it feels like it will burst out in an explosion of blood and guts. The whole room starts to spin. His takes a step backward and his back comes into contact with the back wall. He slowly slides down against the wet tiles until his naked buttocks touch the cold wet floor.

His mind is trying to fight what he is seeing upon the mirror. He confused brain quickly makes the connection. *Mirror*, not *Mira* – that's what she was trying to tell him.

Written in capital letters against the fogged up *mirror*, he sees the word slowly flowing down in ghostly droplets.

LINA

Then the world goes black...

CHAPTER 7

He opens his eyes. The floor feels cold and hard against his naked body. He slowly gets up shivering. His eyes settle on the mirror – only droplets.

His whole right side feels icy and numb. He takes the damp towel from the floor and wraps it around his shoulders. His body is shaking violently as he makes his way to the bedroom.

Lina. The writing. The mirror.

He is not sure now.

John slips on a pair of jeans and a white t-shirt. Friday - casual day. Not that he cares right now anyway.

He checks his watch. 7:47 A.M. He needs a coffee – a double. Hell, maybe even a triple.

The coffee feels hot in his hands. He takes a sip and burns his palate. He can already feel the blister forming with his tongue. His body is starting to feel warmer. He leans back.

Lina. He frowns.

He remembers the writing on the mirror; her name. But now he is not sure whether he just imagined or maybe dreamed it. The whole thing is a blur.

He clearly remembers the dream however. He was trying to get to her. She was sitting at the bar, just like the night before. She was saying Mira, but in fact, he now realizes, it wasn't Mira she was trying to verbalize, it was *Mirror.* She had wanted him to look at the mirror – where her name had appeared. Or had it...

John takes another sip. He is trying to figure out whether he had really seen her name on the bathroom mirror or whether it was just a hallucination. He did have too many drinks in him and he did feel like shit, so anything is possible.

The coffee is getting cold. He hates his coffee cold. He takes the cup to the sink, then jut stands there in a trance, pondering.

What if...it's real. What if the writing on the mirror *is* real. What if it's really her. What if she wrote it. But that would mean...she's dead.

Dead? Nooooo!

John refuses to even imagine that. He grabs the edge of the sink. His knuckles turn white. *Dead. Her ghost. Her ghost wrote the message John. You know that don't you? You know she's dead.*

"Noooooo!" he screams raising his hand, and smashes it against the edge of the sink.

He looks at his hand in shock and shoves it under his armpit. "Shit!!." It feels like its going to explode. He can already feel the broken capillaries forming a bruise beneath the skin.

He lets himself sink to the kitchen floor, his head hanging between his knees.

Lina...please no...

A hopeless, agonizing sob escapes his mouth. Sorrow, pooling from inside, flows out in a sudden surge of tears, his mind trying to fight the obvious truth - the evidence that he saw on the mirror.

His heart tightens in a spasm, skipping a beat. Despair is replaced by rage.

"You bastard!" he screams, spittle landing on the linoleum. "You did it, didn't you! You did it! You killed her you asshole!"

His chest is heaving. Bile rises to his raw throat, making him taste the bitterness inside him.

He shakes his head, refusing to believe it – refusing the harsh evidence on the mirror. "No! No no no! She is alive. I know it! She has to be!"

His breathing slows. He takes a deep breath, trying to calm himself down. He feels his heart slow to a more composed beat. "Yes, she has to be," he sobs. "I will find her and I'll save her from this monster. He will never, *ever*...lay a hand on her again."

He closes his eyes.

She is not dead. He sees her now, lying in his arms, her head resting on his chest. He is kissing the top of her blonde head.

"I will find you my sweet Lina," he whispers. "I'll find you and never let you go..."

CHAPTER 8

"**I**'m telling you it felt so real, her name, Lina, appearing on the mirror."

James takes a drag of his half-consumed cigarette and shakes his head.

"Mate," he says. "I know what you're saying, but it just doesn't make any sense. I don't know, maybe the steam just formed a shape that happened to look like her name?" He pauses for a second, his eyes focused on the glowing tip of his cigarette. "Or maybe," he continues. "You just imagined the whole thing coz you had to much booze in you."

John inhales deeply on his own cigarette and shakes his head.

"Honestly I'm not sure anymore," he says, blue smoke streaming from his nostrils. "You may be right but it feels like it really did happen. And...anyhow, how do you explain the dream then? She did tell me about the mirror in my dream right? So doesn't that make it even remotely possible?"

"I don't know dude. The whole thing seems pretty far fetch. But hey, anything is possible right? I mean I had a friend once who told me that he actually communicated with ghosts; like the real shit, you know, like a seance with a moving table."

John flicks his butt and hears the hiss as it lands into a small paddle on the garage floor. He looks up. "Really?" he frowns. "You really had a friend who talked to ghosts?"

James pulls out a cigarette and offers it to John.

"Yep," he says. "Well that's what he said anyway. I don't think he would be bullshitting me either. We've been friends for quite a while and he would have no reason to..."

John grabs the cigarette, lights it and takes a deep drag – the first is always the best. Not being a heavy smoker, he always gets a nice little head spin on the first inhale.

"Wow!" he says. "That's amazing! I mean if it's real, of course." he squints. "You don't, you know, happen to have his contact? Maybe I could talk to him and find out more?"

"Nahhh," replies James. "It was a while ago and we lost contact. But I do remember him telling me how he had met this ghost. I think Helen was her name, and she had died like a hundred before, hung or something, and that they kinda formed a friendship and he would communicate with her everyday."

"Seriously? That's amazing. So if this is real, it means that ghosts may actually exist!"

"*If*...it's real," James says, extinguishing his own butt between his thumb and index and fishing out another one for himself.

"Yes," John agrees reluctantly. "If...".

James lights his cigarette and ponders for a moment. "Mate," he finally says. "But that means that if the writing on the mirror is real, meaning that it was really made by a ghost, it would also mean that...you know? Lina is...."

John looks up into his friend's eyes, reading what was left unsaid. He looks down, feeling a lump forming in his throat. "Dead. I know," he mumbles biting his lower lip. "I know," he swallows. "But I don't want to believe it. Maybe...maybe there's another explanation. Maybe it wasn't her. Or maybe the whole thing was in my head..."

John looks up. He can feel the lump in his throat getting tighter. He can see James looking at him with piety in his eyes. But he doesn't need pity, he just needs to know that she is OK.

James smiles with uncertainty and lays a sympathetic hand on John's shoulder. "Hey mate, she is probably OK. Really. She is probably at home right now and you are the furthest thing from her mind...and that's a good thing...right?"

CHAPTER 9

John opens the door. He can't stop thinking about her. He was trying to concentrate at work but it's proven impossible. *Lina, Lina, Lina*...her name kept repeating in his head like a broken record. He just couldn't shake it – it was almost driving him mad.

A shower, that's what I need - clear my head.

John hops into the shower. He hasn't fixed the fan and he isn't going to either. He is going to let the bathroom steam up, hoping for another message - another hint.

Leaning against the tiled wall, he lets the steaming hot water run down his back. It feels good. He closes his eyes and sees her face, her eyes, her smile.

"What am I gonna do?" he whispers. "Lina, my sweet Lina."*Where are you? Will I ever see you again? Was that really you on the mirror? Are you alive?*

More questions than answers. No, not more questions than answers; *all* questions and *no* answers.

His body is starting to fill numb. He opens his eyes and notices that the bathroom is already fully steamed up – he can barely make out the soap holder next to the shower head. How long has he been standing in here? Five minutes? Ten? Half an hour? Who knows? Who cares...

The mirror. He must check the mirror!

He steps out of the shower and doesn't bother grabbing a towel. He feels his way to the bathroom door, running his hand along the wet tiled-wall. His foot hits something – hard.

"Ouch!" he cries, leaning down and grabbing his excruciating little toe "You son of a *bitch!*" He notices the small metal door-stopper protruding from the tiled floor. "Damn it! Why would anyone create a *metal* door-stopper in a bathroom! Idiots!"

He slowly gets ups, still holding his toe, and hobbles on one foot to the bathroom door. He grabs the door knob, turns it and opens the door wide.

The steam rushes out of the bathroom in a horizontal cascade as cold air rushes in from the hallway. The sudden decrease in temperature makes every hair on his body stand at attention, as if on parade in front of a general, and his body starts shaking uncontrollably.

John turns his head towards the mirror. He can almost see it now. A message. A sign from the other side. A dreadful evidence to prove that he was right – that she is no longer from this world.

Then he sees it. Both relief and disappointment fill his mind – *nothing.* The mirror is as it should be. Droplets are racing down its length and there is no scrawl defacing his reflection.

He starts to wonder if the 'Lina' that had appeared on the mirror was, as James had said, just an illusion from his alcohol saturated brain. Could she still be alive? Could everything that he thinks happened to her be but a fiddle of his own imagination? The chances of her being alive actually seem much more likely than the murder-mystery-novel idea that she was killed and is lying in a shallow grave somewhere.

John shakes his head, comes out of his trance and grabs a towel on his way to the bedroom.

He now realizes how crazy he's been. *Dead? Ghost? Come on dude.! This is the twenty-first century, not the middle-fucking-ages. Get your shit together and snap out of it!*

"Yea! That's it! Come on!" he shouts. *Do something constructive instead of wallowing in your own imaginative bullshit!*

He puts on a fresh pair of pj's and heads towards the kitchen with determination.

Pasta. Yea that's it. Nothing like a bit of cooking to put things into perspective.

John fills the saucepan with hot water and sets it on the stove. *Yep,* he thinks. *Tomorrow will be a new day and I'm going to do everything I can to find her again.* "And I will! If that's the last thing I ever do!"

John looks down and sees bubbles forming at the bottom of the saucepan. He starts humming as he drops a pinch of salt into the boiling water. He frowns, smiles, and drops in another pinch. *Screw the arteries.*

He grabs a handful of spaghetti, breaks them in two and deposits them into the cloudy, steamy water.

"OK, OK. Now a nice bolognese sauce from Mr. Colman's and Bob's your uncle!"

He opens the cupboard and grabs a can of Mr. Coldman's bolognese sauce. "And who said John can't cook? Mmmmmm?" he laughs.

He digs into the cutlery drawer and his fingers wrap around the can opener. He starts to open the can but hears the water boiling. Worrying that it will overflow, he turns around to lower the heat and he notices the steam rising from the saucepan forming a gray vapor that is starting to find its way to the fan opening atop the window.

He reaches for the string below the fan and sees his own reflection on the kitchen window. Then he sees it...

The Mr. Coldman's bolognese sauce leaves his hand and lands on the kitchen floor, spilling half its content like lava spewing out of a volcano. John takes a step back and hits the kitchen table with the back his legs. His heart is pounding in his chest and a cold sweat starts to covers his body.

His head starts to spin. He grabs the table behind him with both hands to steady himself but his legs buckle under him and cannot support his weight any longer.

His disjointed body falls into a heap, hitting the kitchen floor hard and taking a chair down with it. His wide-opened eyes have never left the the steamed-up kitchen window...

HANDS TABLE

Boiling, foaming water rises above lip of the saucepan and spills onto the floor making small droplets fly up and land on John's hand.

In a split second, the burning sensation reaches his brain

47

and John jerks his hand away, his mind reawakened from the shock.

"Fuck!" he cries out, bringing his hand to mouth and blowing on it. His legs back-pedal as he tries to create a distance between himself and the window. The kitchen table behind him stops him dead in his tracks as the back of his head smashes against its side.

"Shit!"

His burnt hand reaches back and he can already feel the lump forming on his cranium. He shakes his head and slowly manages to reach for the still-sanding chair to his left. He pulls himself up onto the edge and his buttocks finally find reprieve on the yellow checkered cushion.

His hearts starts to slow down, leaving the initial shock behind. John looks at his burnt hand and sees two small blisters surrounded by a bright red rash.

He looks at the window again. Water is now pouring out of the saucepan and spilling onto the floor. Some of it find its way to the burner and extinguishes the flame. John smells the escaping gas, jumps up and quickly turns the gas off.

His heart starts to slow down and his mind becomes coherent again. "Hands table," he says to himself, frowning. *What's that supposed to mean?*

He closes his eyes for a minute, trying to think. And suddenly it hits him. "Of course!" He quickly grabs the chair from the floor and drags it to the end of the kitchen table. He puts both his hands flat on the table.

"That's what you are trying to tell me aren't you?" He feels like an idiot talking to himself but his guts tell him he's not alone. "You want me to put my hands on the table and you are going to talk to me right?"

He can already see it in his mind's eye. The table lifting. The ghost, *her ghost*, trying to communicate with him. Just like in a movie where the room is dark and a medium is trying to communicate with spirits.

Dark...it should be dark.

John quickly gets up and switches the kitchen light off. He grabs a glass on the way back to the kitchen table and fills it with tap water – it could be a long night.

The room is now dark. The glass of water is sitting on the chair right next to him to make sure it won't fall over when...if....the table moves.

John lays both his hands flat on the table. He is sitting at one end. His eyes are focused on the other end.

"Lina," he whispers. "I'm ready my love...talk to me."

He waits...

***

Not a sound can be heard, it's as if the World has ceased to exit. His eye lids feel like they weigh a ton and it takes John a super-human effort just to keep them open.

John looks at clock above the small fridge. 09:38P.M. He's been sitting here with his hands flat on the table for forty minutes, and nothing.

Well, what did he expect? That she was just going to jump up and say, '*Hi John! It's me, Lina! How in the hell are you?*" If that were the case, she would have done that a while ago.

Or maybe he doesn't understand the message on the window? *HANDS TABLE*. What else could it mean? Maybe another enigma? Like when he misunderstood *Mirror* for *Mira*?

John is starting to feel a pain in his lower back. The kitchen chair wasn't exactly made for comfort and he doesn't normally seat on it for that long anyway – his diners always being taken on the couch with the T.V. on. But he doesn't want to move. He can't move...he mustn't.

What if she's almost there? What if she's on the threshold of crossing the void beyond and reaching into his world. If he were to move his hands but an inch, it might break whatever hold she may have. But what if it's all bullshit? What if there are no such things as ghosts? What if it's all in his head?

Oh yea? And what about the writing on the mirror John? Well, I was drunk...Yea? And the window? You weren't drunk then! You were cooking fucking pasta! ... OK OK! Stop it! OK, you win!

John shakes his head, trying to clear out the thoughts that keep invading it. His own pestering thoughts that make him think he might be going crazy.

He feels it before he sees it - a sudden sensation of a feather-like weight invading his body. He feels his fingers press into the table and suddenly the other end of the table starts to slowly rise.

49

John knows that he cannot possibly lift one end of the heavy kitchen table by simply pressing on it. Even if he were to actually seat *on* the table, there is no way that the other end would come up – but it does. Not by much, just an inch or two, but a few inches is all that it needs.

John swallows. He feels scared and excited. Goosebumps appear on his bare arms. Expect for the almost indistinguishable force pushing down on his hands, there is no sensation of being possessed. It's nothing like the movies, no convulsions, no flickering lights, no chairs flying around – none of the bullshit. Just his hands, flat on the table, and the slight rise at the other end making the table stand on two legs at an impossible angle.

John takes a deep breath. The table is not moving, it's just sitting there, with two of its legs up as if waiting for instructions.

"Lina?" John hesitates, his voice shaking. "Errrr...is that you?" He can feel a bead of sweat slowly making its way from his temple down to his collar-bone.

The table's far end slowly rises a little higher and drops back to the ground before lifting again. John feels bile rising from his stomach and swallows it back down.

He needs to find a way to talk her – *if* it is her.

"OK," he says. "Mmmmm...how about you bounce up and down. Once for *yes* and twice for *no*. Is that OK?"

Nothing happens for a few seconds and then the table jounces once – *YES*.

John can feel his palms sweating, but he doesn't want move them, he doesn't want to break the link. His shirt is staring to stick to his back and he can smell his own perspiration.

"Lina," he says, trying to remain calm. "I want to know if it's you. Are you Lina?"

He doesn't know if he is ready for what might come next - the inevitable truth, the certainty, the end of hope...the proof that she is no longer of this World.

John waits for the table to bounce. It's only been a couple of seconds but it feels like an eternity. For a split second he doesn't know if he wants to know and his hands almost come up. But then the table jounces again. Once – *YES*.

The kitchen starts to spin and John sees black spots forming in front of his eyes. His body is sinking into the chair.

Oh no! No! Hands table, I must keep my hands on the table. I can't pass out..not now!

He shakes his head and the kitchen becomes solid again.

Dead. She is dead. There are no more doubts. His vision becomes blurry. He can feel a tear running down his face, and then another. His hands are shaking. He presses them harder against the table top. He has to hold on. He has to know for sure.

"Lina..."

His voice is shaking. "Lina. Are you..." he swallows. "...dead?"

The table doesn't move. It's almost as if it knows John doesn't want to hear the inevitable.

John is still hoping that maybe he got it all wrong, that maybe it's all a horrible nightmare. He's suddenly going to wake up and Lina will be there, right next to him, her head resting on his chest.

A few seconds have gone past and John is suddenly aware that the weight he has been feeling is beginning to leave him. A sense of weightlessness is starting to envelop him and he almost feels as if he is beginning to float up towards the ceiling.

He feels the hair on his head stand as if a slight jolt of electricity is running through his body. The weightlessness continues and he can almost feel his buttocks leaving the chair.

And then she is gone. The table slams back down with a loud bang. John jerks up and looses his balance. For a moment the chair he is sitting on balances on two legs and then the equilibrium is lost and John falls backwards.

His head hits the floor hard and an explosion of pain erupts inside his skull. He feels like he's been hit at the back of the head with a baseball bat.

He tries to open he eyes – stars, black stars. He sees them for the second time, but this time he has no reason to hold on. He lets go...

His last thoughts before darkness takes over. *Lina...is that you?...Lina...*

CHAPTER 10

The small bell above the door jingles as John walks in. The bar is almost empty. The stale beer and second hand smoke feel his nostrils. A grimace crosses his face.

He looks across the bar. He doesn't know how he ended up in here but he knows what he is looking for.

She is there, but unlike the other times, she doesn't seem to have noticed him. She is talking with the bar-tender and laughing.

Maybe he is giving her my phone number? So this is real? John isn't sure what is and what isn't real anymore. He decides that the best way to find out is to go over to her.

He walks slowly. He doesn't want to be noticed. He is afraid that if she notices him she might...disappear.

She is still talking to the bar-tender. She seems absorb and he is praying that she won't look his way until he reaches her – she doesn't.

The bar-tender sees him coming, and smiles.

"What can I get your sir?" he asks. There doesn't seem to be any sense of recognition coming from him. John hesitates. "Errrrr just the usual..." he replies.

"The usual sir?" the bar-tender asks, frowning.

"Never mind. Red label on the rocks please."

His eyes turn to her. She is looking at him, her lips pinched together as if she is trying to recall who he is.

"Lina..." he says, standing next to her, not yet daring to seat.

She looks surprised. "Sorry, I know you?"

She is beautiful, as beautiful as the first night he laid eyes on her. She is wearing the same dress and John tries to hide a smile as he remembers the color of her panties – Russian red. He feels a stir. *Not now John...*

She doesn't seem to remember him. The whole thing feels like deja-vu.

"You don't remember me?" he tries.

She frowns. "I sorry. I not remember. We meet before?"

John feels frustrated but tries not to show it. "Oh, maybe it was a while ago. I think you probably don't remember. Well, anyway. I'm John."

He extends a hand and she takes it.

"Nice meet you John. I Lina," she smiles.

She squeezes his hand once and goes to remove it but he squeezes it on slightly, trying to hold on to the feeling of her skin against his a little bit longer.

She looks into his eyes. Hesitation and...recognition? She pulls a little harder and her hand leaves his, leaving a void where once her touch has been.

A discreet cough from his left. He turns.

"There you are sir, one Johnny Walker on the rocks."

"Oh thanks," he says, taking the drink and giving the bar-tender a generous twenty. "Keep the change." he adds.

The bar-tender smiles. "That's a twenty sir, are you su..."

"Yes," John cuts in. "Just take it..." he smiles back.

I'm here again, he thinks. *No. We are here again.*

He takes a quick sip and turns back to her. "So...Lina. You seem to have a Russian accent, you are from Russia right?"

He hates the idea of having to go back through all the formalities again. He just wants to have her in his arm and make love to her – but he has no choice, losers can't be choosers.

"Yes," she replies. "I know my English not so good. I sorry."

"No, no, no! It's OK, your English is fine! Really..."

He hates this. He needs to move faster. He can feel his arousal just thinking of her naked, riding him.

53

"Well, so you seem to be alone. Do you mind if I join you?"

"No, is OK, please sit. I alone. I suppose to be at friend birthday party but I leave early and come for drink"

"Yes, I know..." John says without thinking.

Lina frowns. "You know?" she asks, biting her lip. "How you know? I just tell you."

John takes a nervous sip. *Damn!*

"Well. I don't know, I mean, I do know..." he blurts out. Lina is looking at him, seeming to enjoy his awkwardness. She is wearing a mischievous lop-sided smile and her lips curl around her straw. He can see her Adam's apple moving up and down as she takes a couple of sips of her Lemon Drop Martini - of course, he knows what shes having.

A bead of sweat rolls down his temple and he wipes it off nervously. He feels like that school-boy again.

"I do know," he says, trying to sounds nonchalant. "Coz, well, you just told me... right?"

Her red lips part from the straw, leaving a small red hallow around it. His eyes cannot leave her lips, her half opened mouth, her bright red lip-stick. Russian red...just like...

"John?"

He snaps back to reality.

"Errr, yes, sorry. Was just day dreaming."

"Is OK. It is late and maybe you tired."

She looks at the clock above the bar and a worried look shadows her face. "Mmmm... almost eleven. Maybe I must go, my husband not happy if I too late."

John swallows. He knows why she is worried. The bastard.

He grabs her hand and this time she doesn't pull back.

"Why don't you stay a bit longer?" he says. "Let me buy you another drink, please..."

Her mesmerizing freckled green eyes meet his. It's almost as if she can read his thoughts, like she knows exactly what he wants – and maybe she does.

"OK John." she smiles. "But just one drink OK?"

***

His hands are shaking as he tries to insert the front door

key of his apartment into the keyhole.

She is so close that he can feel her breath against his neck as she stands, almost too close, behind him in the dark narrow stairway.

Finally he hears the locking mechanism being released as the key turns. He pushes the door open and flicks on the light – too bright.

"Wait," he whispers, switching the light back off and walking over to the couch. His fingers find the switch to the table lamp and the lounge room is illuminated in a hazy glow.

He turns around and she is still standing by the doorway. The light coming in from the corridor find its way through the silk material of her dress and leaves little to the imagination. He can see her outline as if there were nothing there. Her long legs rise all the way to the shadow of her mound as it presses against the fabric of her thin dress, forming a gentle rolling hill. His eyes move up and settle on her perfectly shaped breasts.

His arousal becomes almost unbearable as he remembers the feel of her breasts in his hands and the taste of her womanhood as his tongue found its way inside.

The door closes and the back-light is covered by darkness.

Lina walks over to him and wraps her arms around his neck. Her red, sensual lips meet his as her handbag drops to the floor and her body presses against his.

He feels her moist tongue pushing against his lips and opens them slightly to let her in. His hands move down to her firm buttocks and he pulls her tighter into him. He feels the warmth of her thighs and as her mound settles against his stiffness, he takes a step back and, without leaving her lips, he leans back and lets her body join his on the couch.

His hands start to move down to the sim of her dress, ready to rise it above her head and reveal her red panties.

Her mouth parts from his, leaving him gasping for more.

"John wait..." she whispers, pulling back. "One minute OK? Please me use bathroom first."

John smiles and nods. "Don't take too long, I'll be waiting in the bedroom right next to the bathroom. Champagne?"

She gives him one last sensual kiss, picks up her handbag and starts making her way to the bathroom. She turns the light on and again he can see the curves he will be rediscovering in an instant. He looks down and notices the tent that has formed in his pants - *it might prove challenging to make it to the bedroom on three legs*, he thinks with a mischievous smile.

She turns around and her eyes lock onto his. "Yes please..." she says, licking her slightly smeared red lips.

The bathroom door closes and semi darkness fills the room again. John doesn't move for a minute and then he hears the water running from the bathroom.

"Oh shit..." he reacts. "Champagne!"

He quickly makes his way to the bar where he always keeps a bottle of champagne should the occasion present itself – and today, a celebration is certainly in order.

As he opens the bottle, his mind goes back to the bar. He frowns.

You know this is just a dream, right John? I mean, you do know that you are not going to have sex with her in reality, right?

John shakes his head. *Shut-up! Just shut-up! I don't wanna hear it!* Why does his damned inner-self always have to be so fucking right and spoil the moment.

I don't care. Real or not, it feels damn real enough to me and I'm going to enjoy this.

The bubbles race to the top of the bottle and the cork hits the ceiling with a loud pop leaving a gray mark there. John quickly picks up two flutes and fills them to the rim.

He makes his way to the bedroom and within an instant the two champagne glasses are sitting on the side table and the side lamp is dimmed, just enough for him to still see her gentle curves as her body will be riding waves on him.

He throws open the bed cover.

"Clothes? No clothes?" he asks himself nervously. Again, he feels like a school-kid - she really tends to have that effect on him.

"OK," he decides. "Clothes off, underwear on."

He pulls everything off and puts on a fresh pair of boxers.

He checks his watch - it's been about five minutes. Damn, what is she doing in there? This better be worth it.

He remembers the last time. *Oh, it will be Johnny boy!*

He moves to the left of the bed and changes his mind, back to the right.

He picks up the champagne and notices that his hand is

shaking. He doesn't know how long he will be able to hold it this time, the waiting is killing him.

He takes a sip and puts the glass back on the side table.

His mind starts to wonder. *Is she OK?*

"Lina?" he cries out, trying not to sound too eager. "Are you OK in there?"

Nothing. Just the sound of water.

He frowns. "Lina?" His voice sounds more urgent, almost panicky.

He should go and check. *Maybe she...*

Calm down John. She is just making herself beautiful for you buddy.

He can't calm down, he can feel that something isn't right. *Well, dreams aren't usually right, are they John?*

He has to check.

His head is spinning a little as he gets up too quickly and heads towards the bathroom. The bathroom door is slightly ajar letting out a sliver of light.

Didn't she close the door?

Steam is escaping though the small gap.

John gets to the door and pushes it slowly, not wanting to scare her.

The strong white neon light makes him squint as he peers inside, expecting to find her naked – waiting for him.

His mind can't grasp what he is seeing. Lina is not there but upon the mirror, in droplets that slowly slide down to pool at the base of the sink, he can see the word...

OUIJA BOARD

CHAPTER 11

John opens his eyes. He is looking at the ceiling but it's not the bedroom ceiling, the one he is used to seeing when he wakes up.

The kitchen. He is lying in the kitchen. His head hurts like a bitch. He squints and feels the walnut-size lump at the back of his cranium.

He realizes he is sitting, well, not exactly sitting, but lying/sitting on the kitchen chair that has fallen on the kitchen floor.

He remembers now. Lina. The seance. The table. She talked to him. He thinks it was her, but now he is not so sure. *But the table John...it moved right? If it wasn't her then who? Why would someone, or something, pretend to be her John?*

He knows it's her – it has to be. But some part of him, the sane part, doesn't want to believe it.

He tries to move but his back won't let him - it's crying out in agony at having spent the night on the cold hard floor. He feels his muscles spasm, refusing to respond to the messages his painful head is trying to send them. '*Get up you dip-wit. Come on! Shower. Get up and I'll warm your ass with a nice hot shower*'

Shower? The dream! Lina! The bathroom!

58

The dream. He was waiting for her on his bed, waiting for her to come out of the bathroom, waiting for her to come out so that he could make love to her once again. *Told you it was a dream John...*

The bathroom. The mirror. He remembers the mirror now. There was a message in the dream – *on* the mirror.

Ouija Board John.

Yes, yes that's it! Ouija Board, that was the message. It was her, in the dream. She wants to talk to him, he is sure now. The table. The table was her also. The message on the mirror. It makes sense now, she wants him to build a Ouija board. She wants to talk to him and of course it will be a lot easier with a Ouija board!

"I have to make a Ouija Board..." he grunts.

With a gargantuan effort, his back screaming in agony, John manages to put his weight on his elbows. The chair he's supposed to be sitting on is resting on its back and he manages to roll to one side and get himself on all fours.

He reaches for the chair in order to get it back up but his back doesn't like the side-way movement. *Later...*

He tries to get up but it feels like his muscles and joints have given up and gone on strike for the unfair working conditions. He gives up and crawls to the bathroom on all four.

He makes it the sink and grabs the edge to pull himself up - at least his arms are still working.

His reflection is looking back at him - white as a ghost - he feels like he is the one who's on the other side. There is dried up saliva at the corner of his lips and dark half-moon circles under his eyes.

He opens the shower curtain and steps into the cubicle. He lets the hot water run for a while until he can barely get under it. The water feels good and he lets it stream down his back and at the back of his head. His senses are starting to reemerge and his mind starts to clear up.

The Ouija board appears in his mind. Cardboard. He needs cardboard and a black felt pen. A triangle. He needs a triangle also.

He can see it now. Alphabet on top in a semi-circle and numbers, zero to nine, at the bottom. The triangle will be in the middle. His finger resting lightly on it and waiting. Waiting for her...

***

The Ouija Board is rudimentary but it will do. John didn't want to waste time making it look pretty, he just wants it to be functional.

He is now sitting cross-legged on the carpet in the lounge room with his index finger resting lightly on the little cardboard triangle. He's colored two of the tips red – one pointing up towards the letters and the right hand bottom tip pointing towards the numbers.

A glass of water is sitting next to him. He doesn't know how long it will take and he wants to make sure he doesn't have to break the communication - if it ever comes that is. He's even made sure that he's emptied his bladder before settling down.

It's been twelve minutes already and still nothing. Maybe the Ouija Board is not properly made? He should have checked on the internet on how to make a proper one but he didn't think that ghosts would care one way or the other. Or maybe the letters and numbers should be positioned differently?

John shakes his head. Never-mind, what's done is done, wait and see.

"Lina?" he whispers, thinking that talking too loud might scare her away. "Are you there? Well, I'm ready. Let me know if you are here OK? I'm ready..."

He doesn't know whether he should be doing something special. Sometimes they have candles in movies. Does that help? He made sure that he dimmed the lights to make it more cozy. It seems that ghosts like darker rooms and coziness. *Right...and why don't you put on some soft music, a bottle of bubblies and a few pillows while you're there John? You know she ain't gonna talk to you right? You know it's all in your head and its all bullshit, don't you?*

"Shut-up..."

Did his finger just move? He definitely felt a twinge...or maybe a small cramp from staying in the same position?

There it is again. He can feel his finger pulling slightly towards the 'H'. He relaxes. He mustn't tense, maybe it's holding her back.

The finger moves. Slowly and hesitantly at first as if it...*she* doesn't know how to control it.

"Lina?" he risks. "Lina? Is that you?" *Let her talk you dumb-ass!*

It reaches the 'H' then goes back to the center before moving to the 'I'.

John frowns. The finger is now back in the center and has stopped moving.

'H', 'I'.

"Hi!" he exclaims. "Lina. It's you? Can you tell me it's you?"

The fingers moves, without hesitation this time and it decisively lands on 'Y', 'E', 'S'.

"Yes," John confirms. He takes a long, deep breath before asking the inevitable question – the one that's been eating him inside since the day after that unforgettable night with her.

"So..." he hesitates. "This, means you are -" he can't get the last word out. He doesn't have to, the finger has already started moving towards the inevitable 'Y'.

'YES'.

He tries to hold it together. He has his answer now. He feels his stomach sink and nausea rises to his throat.

Lina, his beautiful Lina is gone. She is no longer part of this World. He must hold it together, nothing will bring her back. He needs to find out what happened. He knows it's *him*, her husband, that bastard.

He swallows, trying to hold back the tears. The lump in his throat makes it hard for him to speak.

"It's *him* isn't it? It's your husband right? He....killed you..." he says, his voice shaking with sadness and anger.

'YES'.

A tear runs down his face, followed by another. *Not now John, there is time for this later. Focus on her for now John. She needs you.*

"Wh...what happened?" John asks.

'ARGUE'

"Argument. OK, is that because you were late?"

'YES'

John cannot believe it. "OK..." he says, feeling the heat building up inside him like a hot furnace. "And...he killed you for an argument? Because you were late? What the fu! " he shouts.

His finger moves faster now.

'ACCIDENT'

John tries to calm down. *Accident my ass.*

"Accident," he repeats, trying to understand. "He killed you by accident? How? What happened Lina? This is crazy!"

He can feel the room spinning. There is a tiny sense of relief from knowing what happened, but at the same time, a sense of loss and despair. All this time he thought he might have been able save her from this monster, but now the horrible truth is starring at him right in the face.

Yet it's not really news now, is it? Inside he already knew - he just didn't have the courage to admit it to himself.

His finger starts moving again, more slowly this time. Almost as if she were telling him it was OK, as if she were trying to calm him down.

'PUSH,' a pause. 'BATHROOM'

John starts to picture it in his head. Lina coming home late. Her husband still awake, waiting. The heated argument. Her, running up the stairs, heading for the bathroom. He catches up to her, grabs her, pushes her...she falls down and breaks her neck. Her body a heap, her neck twisted at an impossible angle. Her lifeless eyes starring at the ceiling.

"Lina..." he sobs.

He can see her eyes now, as they had been that night, looking at him. How beautiful she had looked when he was holding her in his arm after they had made love, after that unforgettable night. And now those beautiful eyes, covered in a white veil. The veil of the dead - the veil of eternal blindness.

"Lina," he says, struggling to keep his voice steady. "Lina, my love...I'm so sorry," he cries. It's..."

His body starts to shake uncontrollably. An agonizing cry escapes his opened mouth. "I'm so sorry! It's my fault!"

Tears, mixed with mucus, flow down in a translucent mixture of pain. The haze that had shadowed her eyes, as her heart had stopped beating, now covers his as if to let him share the agony of her death.

His hand moves and his finger jumps up.

"Oh no! Lina?" he cries.

He puts his finger back on the triangle.

"Lina? Babe? You still there?" he asks, his cloudy eyes starring at his unresponsive finger. "Sorry! I'm sorry babe, my finger moved...Lina? Hello?"

Nothing.

He tries to calm himself down. He needs her back. He needs to understand. His feels his chest tightening up as if a vice is trying to squeeze out the last few remaining tears that flow down his face.

"Lina, please..." he begs. "I'm sorry. I didn't mean to move my finger. It's just, that bastard, what he did to you. I'm sorry, I was angry. Please babe...come back to me."

John has all his focus on his finger now, willing it to move, hoping that his concentration might be able to help Lina reestablish the connection.

He takes a drink, making sure not to move his finger from the triangle, and looks at the clock. It's been about four minutes since he has broken the connection. He decides to try a few more minutes but knows that she won't be back, not tonight anyway.

It's been over half an hour now and he can feel all the muscles on his lower back begging for him to get up. The sitting on the hard carpet and the seance have taken their toll and his cramping legs and back are letting him know.

John reluctantly pulls his finger away from the Ouija Board. He cannot make himself move and just leans back on the carpet.

His eyes are focused on the bare light-bulb sitting in the middle of the ceiling. Is she looking down at him?

He can feels his eye lids getting heavy. He doesn't want to move. He wants to stay near the Ouija Board – near her.

He turns his head and gently puts his finger on the triangle. He feels closer to her now, just like that night when she was lying next to him.

His eyes finally close. "Goodnight my love..." he whispers.

CHAPTER 12

"Dead? What do you mean dead?"

John takes a sip of his one-two-many coffee. He hasn't been able to get much sleep after the Ouija Board seance last night and the lump at the back of his head is killing him.

He can still see the Ouija Board and his finger moving to the letter 'Y' before he even had the chance to finish asking her if she was dead.

"She told me...I mean she said *yes* when I asked her."

James shakes his head. "Dude, I know you probably *think* she did but it doesn't make any sense. Gees, I don't know, maybe you were still dreaming after you hit your head?"

John touches the lump at the back of his cranium and winces. "Buddy, I know how crazy all this sounds but you really have to believe me. I mean, why the hell would I lie to you?"

James sighs. "Hey, I'm not saying that you're lying. What I'm saying is that maybe, just *maybe*, and just like you dreamed of sleeping with her and saw the mirror, is it possible that the Ouija Board seance was also just a dream?"

John looks around and leans forward. "A dream? How can it be a dream since I woke up on the carpet with the board right next to me?"

James takes a sip of his lukewarm coffee and scratches his head. "Well...maybe you *did* make the Ouija Board and tried to use it and after a while, you know, fell asleep. I mean why not? You did hit your head before that and so..."

John doesn't need this. He needs his friend to believe him. He knows it wasn't a dream and he knows he was 'talking' to her. "Please, believe me. You're the only one I can talk to about this and the only one who can help me figure this thing out."

John sees his friend's shoulders relax in a sign of resignation. "Fine. OK, let's say it's true then. Let's just say that you really did speak to her. Let's assume that ghosts really do exist and that you were speaking to one, which happens to be Lina, *and* that she told you that she's dead." James shakes his head. "So let's just assume all this is true, although, you do know how crazy the whole thing sounds right?"

John rubs his eyes. The coffee isn't helping much and trying to prove to James that he hasn't gone over the edge doesn't make it any easier.

He remembers Lina. He remembers that first night. He remembers the Ouija board. He swallows. The tight lump in his throat doesn't want to go away. He wants to scream, he wants to let it all out and scream at how unfair this is, how unfair this is for her and how unfair this is for him. He doesn't want to be here with James, talking to him over a cup of coffee about her, about her as a ghost. He will never see her again. He will never hold her in his arms again.

His lower lip starts to quiver. He swallows again. He can feel a tear forming, his vision becoming blurry. He looks up at his friend.

"Buddy," he manages, his voice shaking. "This is horrible..." The tear finds its way down and he wipes it off absently with the back of his hand.

James looks worried. He puts his hand on his friend's shoulder.

"Mate," he says, sympathy in his voice. "I know it's hard. I mean, I can't even imagine what you're going through. If it were me, I would...hell, I don't even know what I would do."

John sighs, trying to pull himself together. "Yes," he sniffs and uses a napkin to wipe his nose. He swallows. The lump is still there. "I have to do something. I know it's too late. I know that, but I have to make it right. He can't get away with it. That bastard did this to her and I have to make sure he pays for it. He has to pay for taking her life."

James lets go of his friend's shoulder and takes a sip of coffee. He grimaces and puts it back down. "So, what you gonna do mate? Call the police?"

"I don't know. I mean...I mean I'm not sure."

"What do you mean you're not sure? I think that would be the right thing to do right? He has to pay and go to jail for what he did."

John shakes his head. "You don't understand. What's that going to achieve? How can they even prove it? I mean I only know her first name, plus I don't have any idea where she lives. And even if the police did get involved, they'd probably think I'm a total nut-case. What am I even supposed to tell them? 'Oh yes...well, I was talking to her ghost and she told me she was killed by her husband?' Shit dude, I'm probably the one who's gonna end up behind bars for insanity..."

James frowns. "Yes...well, I see what you mean. I mean, I'm your friend and I'm having a hard time with this, so I can't even imagine what the cops are gonna think."

"Anyway buddy, I need to do something, I can't just let him get away with this."

James picks up his coffee. "That's cold, want another one?" he says, getting up and heading to the cashier.

"Nah," John replies. "I'm good thanks."

He picks up another napkin and wipes his nose. He looks around. The canteen is almost empty; its too nice a weather to be sitting indoors for lunch, thank God for that. At least there isn't anyone to see him look like shit with a snotty nose.

James comes back with two steaming cups.

"Here you go mate. It'll do you good," he smiles. "You really look like shit..."

John takes his fifth cup gratefully and fakes a pinched-lipped smile. "Ha ha thanks," he says. "You really know how to make a guy feel better."

James takes the opposite seat. "So what now? Seriously. What you gonna to do now dude?"

John closes his eyes. He is tired, but he knows that this is not the end. In fact, he knows it's only the beginning - it's obvious that Lina wants something from him.

He opens them again and ponders for a moment with his chin resting in his hand. "I'm not sure," he finally says. "But what *I'm* sure off is that she wants something from me."

66

"Yes," James agrees. "If all this is what it appears to be, and no matter how crazy it seems, it looks like she's trying to reach out to you. Maybe you should try to talk to her again and see what she wants."

John takes one last sip of his coffee. "I'll do that buddy. Well, I'll try to anyway...all depends on her. I need to see what she wants and I'm also not going to let that bastard get away with what he did. He took her life and he'll pay for that, one way or another."

James gets up and rests his hand on John's arm. "Let me know what happens dude. And...well, if it makes any difference, I believe you, and I'll support you. Whatever it takes mate."

John forces a smile. "Thanks buddy. I appreciate it. I really can't go through this alone..."

CHAPTER 13

The day has been impossibly long. All he could think about was Lina. He couldn't wait to get home so that he could talk to her again.

He grabbed some McDonald's on the way. Not exactly the kind of thing that will do much good to his middle section but at this stage he really doesn't give a shit.

The stage is set. The lights are dimmed and he has a glass of water and a thermos filled to the rim with dark, strong coffee - could be a long night.

His finger has only been resting on the triangle for about ten minutes now but it already   feels like an eternity.   He wonders how long he will have to wait. Is it so difficult for her to communicate with him? How does it feel to be a ghost? He can't even imagine. He always had doubts about ghosts but now he knows, but honestly, he wishes he didn't.

A movement. Yes, he feels it. Just a slight twinge but yes, that definitely wasn't his doing.

Again. A little stronger this time.

He swallows. "Lina? Is that you?"

His finger slowly slides to the 'Y' then 'E' and 'S'.

His heart accelerates and he tries to keep his finger light but steady. "OK, I got it. Mmmmm we don't have to use the alphabet for yes and no. Let's just use Y for Yes and N for no. It will be faster that way. OK?"

'Y'

Wow...this is real. I'm really talking to her now.

"Errrrr. OK. Mmmmmmm where do we start? Well I'm sorry, maybe I should have prepared some questions. Anyway...how are you?"

How are you? What the hell John! She is dead! How do you think she is?

'O','K'

He closes his eyes. *Come on John, get your shit together. Make it count.*

"I'm sorry. That was a stupid question. I guess the whole idea of talking to you is still overwhelming. I...I just never thought that I would see you again. Well, not exactly see you but...you know..."

His finger start moving faster now as if the connection is stronger.

'IS OK'

John shakes his head in disbelief. "Wow. This is so amazing. I still can't believe I'm talking to you."

'ME 2'

He slowly opens the lid of the thermos with one hand. He made sure he didn't screw it on tight so that he would be able to use one hand only. He takes a sip of the strong brew.

"OK. Well, guess it's better that I ask some questions and you try to reply as simply as possible. Deal?"

'K'

"Sooooo, from what you said last time, it was your husband who...took your life."

'Y'

The lump in his throat is back. It feels like an apple is stuck in there and he has to keep swallowing to bring it down, but it won't budge.

"Well," he chokes. "What happened?"

His finger doesn't move.

He frowns. Has he lost her already? Then he realizes. "Oh sorry! My bad. Simple questions..."

69

He takes a sip of water. "OK, let's see. You came home and he was angry that you came late. How am I doing so far?"

'Y'

"Right. So...you had an argument. And then it got...physical"

'Y AND N'

John scratches his head. "Right. Mmmmm...this is not so easy. How about you explain it to me in simple words without worrying about grammar OK?"

'OK'

John takes another sip of the steaming hot coffee. He looks down and notices the steam rising up, merging itself with the cool air until it becomes one. He wonders what it's like to be a ghost – to be Lina. Can she see him as people see each-other? Ghosts don't have a body, eyes, ears...how do they see, hear, smell? How does she use him? How does she move his finger? He can't even feel her inside him, yet she is there...

His finger moves. John doesn't bother putting the lid back.

'ARGUE SCREAM ME BATHRM CRY HE COME SCREAM PUSH ME HIT HEAD SINK...DIE'

The words have come one by one and John is replaying the scene in his head. It was in the bathroom that it happened. That bastard pushed her while she was in the bathroom, probably cleaning her face after crying. He can see it now. The fear in her eyes, his enraged face close to hers, his hands on her shoulders, the final, violent push that ended her life. The bathroom, all white, expect for the bright crimson liquid spilling from the gash in her head, her life draining out of her in a pool of blood, her empty eyes staring in horror and shock at the ceiling and the life slowing vanishing from them until they are nothing but white orbs in an empty shell.

John is sitting in a trance, his eyes opened but seeing nothing. The image of her face, in the bathroom, is all he can see now. The light that has faded from her eyes and the white embryonic membrane that has replaced it.

The finger moves again and he comes out of his trance. It moves towards the J.

'JON U OK?'

He shakes his head. "Oh Lina. Yes...no, I don't know. I mean, this is horrible. What happened to you. What he did to you."

'Y'

"Babe, I mean Lina..."

Finger moves suddenly. 'BABE OK'

Even-though he doesn't feel like smiling, a tiny smile crosses his face. *Babe*. He likes the sound of that. It makes him feel closer to her.

Closer to her? Who are you kidding John? She is a ghost for Christ's sake! A fucking ghost! She is dead John! D, E, A, D, dead! She is not human!

Shut up! Just shut-up! She is not just a ghost! She is Lina! She is the amazing girl I met in the bar. She is not just a...ghost! So shut-up!

'JON?'

John frowns. "Lina? You...you heard me? I mean you heard what I was thinking? You can hear my thoughts..."

'Y'

"Wow! I...I don't know what to say. It's just my...subconscious. It's always so freaking negative and trying to put me down and...and trying to make me see everything in black and white. But babe, to me you are not *just* a ghost. You are that beautiful, wonderful woman I met at the bar. Babe...I'm so, so sorry for what happened to you."

'N'

"Let me finish please," he chokes guiltily. "It *is* my fault. The reason that you came home so late was because of me. It's because I wanted you to come back to my place. I knew that you were married and I was selfish. All I could think of was you in my arms and how wonderful it would be. I'm so sorry Lina. It's my fault that he...he..."

John feels his finger press harder into the triangle and a tingle, almost like an electrical shock, shoots up his arm.

'NO!'

He barely manages to keep his finger on the board.

'I WANT U ALSO NOT U FAULT"

John looks at his finger. His link to Lina. It is shaking. He uses his left hand to steady his wrist and tries to calm himself down. He doesn't want to loose her again – not now.

"Oh babe. I'm sorry. I don't know what to say. I can't help but feel guilty for what happened to you..."

'HAPPEN ONE DAY ANYWAY'

John recoils. "What do you mean? Like he was going to kill you? He planned this?"

'N BUT INEVITABL'

"Inevitable? You mean he hit you before and this was bound to happen?"

'Y'

John feel his anger mounting inside, this is so crazy. "But...but why didn't you leave him? I mean, if he was violent? Why didn't you just leave?"

'MARRY NO MONEY'

"Yes, I know you were married. But I mean, I don't know, couldn't you call a friend, a sister, you parents, go back to Russia?"

'N PASSPORT N MONEY STUK'

John closes his eyes. He has heard stories before where abused, married women stay in a relationship because they have no choice. They are imprisoned in a world of violence and abuse and they have no way of escaping; either because they have no-where to go or because they are too ashamed, thinking that it is their fault and that their husband has every right to punish them. But this is wrong, John thinks, so damn wrong.

"So...he was always violent?"

'Y'

"Lina I'm so sorry. You should have gone away before...before..."

'CANT'

"I know. I understand babe, you were stuck."

'Y'

John doesn't know what to say. He understands and yet he can't stop feeling that this is his fault. She has died because of him, because he was bloody selfish, because he knew that she was married and he still went for her. But then, her marriage was screwed anyway and she had wanted him just as much as he had wanted her.

Yes John, try to make yourself feel better. That's it, not your fault now is it? Just coz you couldn't keep your dick in your pants.. Lina is dead because of you...and you know it.

Another jolt. 'STOP!'

"But babe..."

'NO JON! NOT U FAULT OK?'

John sighs. Maybe she's right. Maybe what happened was inevitable.,with or without him being in the picture, it would have happened...eventually.

His mouth feels like sandpaper. He takes a sip of water. "I'm sorry," he says. "Maybe you're right. Maybe it wouldn't have made any difference whether I met you or not."

'IT DOES'

John doesn't understand. "It does?"

'Y'

"How?"

'BCOZ IT WI-'

The finger stops moving. "Lina?"

One minute. Nothing. "Lina? You there babe?"

Nothing.

"Oh no...babe, please come back."

His finger doesn't move. John feels a void deep inside. He hardly felt the barely discernible weight that was bearing down him when they were talking, but now that she's gone, the loss is unbearable. He feels like an empty shell, cast aside after it's inside has served it's purpose.

He knows she's gone.

"Lina?..."

CHAPTER 14

John is sitting at his desk, trying to concentrate on the chart in front of him. It's impossible, something, or rather someone, is totally filling his mind. He realizes that he hasn't stopped thinking about her since the day he met her.

He pulls out his calculator and his fingers do the math – 86400, that's how many seconds he's been thinking about her everyday. Well, he did sleep but then again, he did dream about her also...so that should count right?

What the hell John? What are doing to yourself? You are obsessed with a damn ghost!

Not just a ghost damn you! It's Lina!

Yea but...

Shut-up.

John looks down at the flowchart. An algorithm. A process filled with different kinds of boxes that are joined by arrows that represent inputs and outputs and the decisions that have to be made in order to find a solution to a given problem.

He is looking but not seeing. All he can see is Lina.

Solutions to a problem. Lina. The big problem that is now filling his days and requires a solution. He misses her like crazy.

He looks at his watch – 09:10 A.M. It's going to be a long day before he's able to talk to her again.

He sighs. He looks around. He can hear the endless stroking of keys on overused keyboards. A laughter on his right; someone on the phone sharing a joke with his sweetheart maybe? God he misses her...

Problem...have to wait till tonight. Solution... says who?

Yes, there must be a solution. Is there a way he can talk to her whilst at work? A method in which he would just be able to sit here and talk to her without anyone knowing?

He looks at his keyboard. Letters, numbers. Could she use his fingers to type? He frowns, his eyes narrowing to two narrow slits. He feels the keyboard and tries to slide his fingers from key to key. No, the keyboard doesn't feels smooth enough for his fingers to slide around, and it would also mean that he would have to be at his desk whenever he would want to talk to her.

There has to be a better solution. He looks at his fingers sitting on the keyboard – fingers, or rather *finger,* singular.

Yes! That's it! He smiles and looks around, pleased with himself. Problem? Solution! No wonders he is such a fucking good Analyst!

His finger! He could just put it on the desk, or anywhere really. Maybe even on his lap, under the desk, so that nobody can see. If she is able to move a table or move his hand on a Ouija Board, she should have no problem simply taping his finger up and down.

He can see it now. So simple. Tap once for yes, twice for no. For a more elaborate conversation, just use the alphabet. Maybe start with a tap meaning consonant and then go through the consonants as in tap, tap, tap or maybe start with two taps for vowels and the just five taps to represent the vowels.

He slaps his head. Damn! He's a god damn genius!

"OK," he says to himself. *Quick bathroom break to settle the nerves and let's give it a shot.*

He walks over to the bathroom and the big, stupid smile on his face shows the excitement bubbling inside him. He feels like a bottle of champagne with its cork ready to pop. Susan, his coo-worker, looks up, frowns and gets back to her ceaseless, meaningless task. *Yep,* John thinks, *so much for the cycle of life. Wake, work, eat, shit, sleep and...do it all over again until you're six feet under... Well, not me babe!*

Business done, he quickly walks back to his desk, trying his best to keep a straight face – damn hard when the spring in your step makes it look like you can't wait to get back to your job! *As if...*

He sits down and gets comfortable. He puts his left hand on the chart and assumes a deeply-concentrated facial expression so as not to get disturbed.

He pulls the chair closer to his desk, so that his legs are hidden under it, and rests his right hand flat on his thigh.

OK, he thinks, *now wait.*

It's almost instant this time. Almost as if she knew what he was about to do, and maybe she did – she *can* read his mind after all.

His index finger comes up slowly. It's a weird feeling, almost as if it were numb and someone was lifting it, expect that he can still feel his finger but not the someone.

Lina? Is that you? he thinks.

One tap.

OK. great! Well lets keep it simple OK? One tap for yes or OK, two for no or not OK. If you want to use the alphabet, three taps and then follow with one tap if you want to use consonants and two taps for vowels. Then just tap, tap, tap and I'll follow in my head. Deal?

Tap.

Well, how are you? I mean, how are you under the circumstances?

Tap.

I'm OK too. Well not really actually. I'm sorry to disturb you but... 'can you disturb a ghost?'...' *I missed you and...I couldn't wait for tonight to see you again. I mean, talk to you ...again.'*

Three taps. 'ME TO MIS U HAPY U ERE'

Oh babe. I'm so happy also, so happy that we are able to talk here. Well, can I ask you some questions? Not about what happened, I just want to know more about you.

Tap.

John looks around to make sure that no one is approaching his desk. No one, good. He wants to be alone with her.

Mmmm OK, well, what's it like?

Tap, tap,tap.

'WAT IS WAT LIKE'

Sorry, I mean what is it like up there. I mean beyond?

'HARD 2 SAY'

What do you mean?

'U WONT UNDESTAN'

Try me...

'NO TIME N NO SPACE'

A deep furrow forms between John's eyebrows. He doesn't really understand what she means but if it is what he's thinking then the whole concept seems totally crazy.

What do you mean – no time and no space? Like space and time don't exist?

Tap.

"Wow!" he exclaims a bit too loudly, making the colleague sitting on his left give him a hard stare as he if he's totally lost it, and...well, maybe he really has, he is talking to a ghost after all.

"Wow!" he whispers this time. *You mean that time, like, you know clocks, twenty-four hours in a day and like distance like from here to...I don't know, maybe France, don't exist?*

Tap.

John cannot wrap his head around this one. How can life, or in this case, death, or maybe a subconscious-life, exist without time and space? He always had some idea that a ghost would simply be a lost soul and that's this. But the idea that the whole concept of life after death would be under a totally different universe that completely defies the laws of physics is mind boggling! Maybe he misunderstood...

"OK," he whispers, wanting to make sure that she really understands what he is asking instead of thoughts coming out of his head. "So you mean that, for example, if after this conversation, we don't talk until this evening or...let's say next year, it makes no difference to you? I mean time-wise?

Tap,Tap, Tap.

'YES NO DIFFERENCE TIME N SPACE N DISTANCE NOT EXIT'

John leans back on his chair and scratches his head with his left hand, making sure that his right one stays firmly on his thigh. Thoughts run through his head, trying to even imagine what a world like this would be like.

OK, OK, this too crazy, and you are right, I totally don't even come close to understanding a World without the basic laws of physics. Mmmmm...does this also mean that you can basically travel anywhere you want at the blink of an eye?

'YES BUT U NOT UNDESTAN'

John is lost for words. This idea of Lina in such a place is insane. She must be so scared. How do you get used to being there after you die? Wouldn't you go crazy? It's like...suddenly being able to float in outer-space naked and being able to breathe! And that's putting it mild, at least space is something we partially understand! This is really out of this world – literally!

He can feel his heart pounding in his chest and his undershirt is starting to be impregnated with the sweat that is pouring out of his skin. He can smell his own musky odor. His nostrils flair in response.

"Lina," he whispers. "Are you OK? I mean, are you OK in this place? I can't even imagi-"

Tap.

He closes his eyes.

Bzzzzzz....Bzzzzzz...

He jumps up and his hand suddenly falls off his thigh. *Oh no! Not again!*

Bzzzzzz....Bzzzzzz...

"Shit! Damn it! Why now!" He picks up the phone. "Yes?" he shouts, annoyed, into the mouth-piece.

"Wow! Dude! What's up? You OK?" It's James.

John takes a breath, trying to calm himself down. "Yes, yes, I'm sorry," he says. "I'm just...sorry, you caught me at a bad time."

"Sorry dude, but aren't you supposed to be at the status meeting as in five minutes ago? You coming?"

John looks at his watch. "Oh shit! It's ten-o-five already! OK, OK, I'm coming. Room 2 right?"

He hears James sigh at the other end. "Yep, better be quick before Margaret shows her face, you know what she's like..."

John hangs up and grabs his flowchart. He is just about to get up and stops.

"Sorry babe," he apologizes. *I'll see you tonight.*

But then he remembers, a minute or a week won't make any

difference to her, it's him who is already missing her like crazy...

CHAPTER 15

A quick bite to eat, a freshly brewed coffee and a bottle of water. John is ready.

He decided that if this were to become a nightly habit, he should at least make himself comfortable should he fall asleep after the session. He realizes that talking with Lina on the Ouija Board isn't really tiring while he is doing it but his body does feel pretty drained afterwards, thus comfort is of the essence.

The sturdy little adjustable table he picked up on his way home is perfect and it almost seems like it was made for his seance – just enough space for the board at the center and his water and coffee next to it. It even has enough space for a small packet of cookies should he get the munches during their conversation. The only problem, of course, is toilet breaks. He'll have to think of a way to fix that. Problems...solutions. Yep! That's John!

Lights are dimmed and his finger is sitting lightly on the triangle. Again, it doesn't take long – almost as if she's been waiting for him as much as he was eager to meet her.

'HI JON'

John smiles. "Helloooooo. How are you?"

'GOOD U?'

"Well," he sighs. "Been a long day. After our little talk this morning, all I could think about was coming back home so that we can meet again. I know it might be too early to say this but honestly...I've missed you."

'ME 2'

He opens the thermos' cap with his left hand and takes a sip of coffee. The warm brew descends, warming him inside. Perfect, he thinks. He feels like in a cocoon. The room is warm and cozy and it's just the two of them.

"Hi, let me ask you something. Errrr, how do you do it?"

'DO WAT?'

OK, OK, be more explicit John. "I mean, how do you talk to me? Like, how do you make my hand move? Do you, you know, get inside me or something?'

'NO PSYCHIC COMMUNICATION'

John holds his chin, pondering. "You mean, there is nothing physical? It's just your mind controlling my hand?"

'YES I GOST SO HAVE MIND'

John can't really get it. But then a thought is nothing physical as such. "So you mean a Ghost is basically a....floating thought?"

'FLOATING SOUL SPIRIT INDIVIDUAL'

"Mmmmmm OK. So I guess a soul must be different from a thought. So souls have thoughts, right? I guess it's like people. We are individuals and we have thoughts.

'Y '

John takes a drink of water. The room is starting to feel a bit warm. "Right, I'm starting to get this. So basically, the only difference between humans and ghost is our...shape, our physical form.

'GOSTS R HUMAN JUST OTHE SHAPE AND DIMENSION'

"Oh yes, I forgot, there is also this dimension thingy where time and space don't exist, right?"

'Y'

John nods slowly. The whole thing is starting to make more sense. Basically, ghosts and humans...people, are the same. Well mentally anyway. The rest, the world she lives in and the physics of her world are totally different. He still can't come close to perceiving a whole universe without time, space or distance but it's something that he'll just have to accept.

The finger suddenly moves.

'JON SOMTHIN MUST TELL U'

He swallows and a knot forms in his stomach. From experience, when a woman says that she has to tell you something, it can't be good. "OK," he says. "Go ahead."

'I NO SUPOS TALK TO U'

The knot tightens, this can't be good. "Wow....what do you mean you're not suppose to talk to me?"

'GOST NO SUPOZ TALK 2 PEOPLE'

He knew this was too good to be true. A bead of sweat forms high up on his forehead and he feels a drop flow down his left temple. "So..." he hesitates, not wanting to come out with it, not wanting to find-out. "This means, we can't talk anymore?"

"N"

Relief fills his body. "So, what do you mean? We can still talk?"

'I BREAK RULE'

John doesn't like this at all. Breaking rules. He can't help but feel guilty. Isn't it enough that she died because of him? And now he is going to create more trouble for her by making her do something she's not supposed to. What would they do to her? Hell? Worse?

Oh guilty now...are we John? Well, you didn't feel so guilty when you knew that she was married and still brought her back to your apartment, now did you John? And...you certainly didn't feel guilty when she was riding you on the couch...now did you John? And you definitely did not feel guilty when you asked her for her phone number so you could fuck her again! DID YOU JOHN?!!

A sudden jerky movement is felt as his finger jumps to the 'S'.

'STOP!'

He jerks back. He forgot that she could read his mind. "What will happen if you talk to me? If you break the rules? I'm worried babe...what will they do?"

'NOT SURE BUT WORTH'

"Are you sure?" he says anxiously. "I mean, I want to talk to you and be with you but I don't want you to get into trouble just because of me."

'SURE'

John inhales deeply and forces the air out of his lungs. He doesn't feel comfortable with this. But then, now that he's finally been able to find a way to talk to her, he doesn't want to give it up so easily.

The room feels warmer. It must be him. He can feel sweat running down his armpits and slowly find its way to his waistband. He can smell himself - the smell of disgust and guilt, the smell of remorse of what he has done and what he continues to do for his own selfish gratification. He rubs his eyes. He is tired. No matter how he feels, there is no going back now, there is only going forward.

'PLS JON I WANT B WITH U DONT STOP'

She has read his mind. She has felt his guilt. She doesn't want him to stop and deep inside, he doesn't want to either. He knows how he feels, even-though he doesn't want to admit it, it's already too late. The whole idea is totally disturbing and insane but he can't stop thinking of her. The fact that she is a ghost would, to anyone, feel like he's totally lost it, but to him she is not just a ghost, an entity out of this world, to him, she is Lina. Lina the beautiful woman he has made love to and the one that has filled his dreams ever-since. How can he go back now? How can he continue knowing that she is there, waiting for him? And what about him? It's not just her who needs him but he who also needs her just as much. He knows it, as much as he feels the increasing beat of his own heart when he thinks of her, he knows that he cannot let go of her.

"I wont," he finally says. "Babe, I won't let you go. It's so crazy, I've only met you once and I can't stop thinking of you. You fill every minute of my day and my mind is filled with your image all the time. I don't understand it. In fact, I don't want to even try to understand it because it would seem so wrong. But inside babe, I know it's right and I know that I want nothing more than to be with you.

He looks at his finger. Nothing. An emptiness fills him and a sense of desolation replaces the sense of guilt and insanity. Maybe she has given up on him. Maybe she just can't do it...

The triangle moves.

'MUST GO JON'

A pause. He waits -

'I THINK'

83

Another pause, longer this time. He thinks the connection has been broken. And then...

'I LOVE U'

Then his finger leaves the triangle.

CHAPTER 16

John is lying in bed, thinking of the last words she had said to him before breaking the connection. *I love you.*

He is still thinking of their conversation. There is so much more that he wanted to ask her, so much more that he wanted to tell her. He wanted to share his dreams with her. Had she really been there, in his dreams, or, were they nothing more *but* dreams? But if they were, how did she manage to reach him? He is pretty certain that initially the dreams had been real, but it also seems like she's been able to get into them and interact with him, giving him subtle hints and clues as to how to get in contact with her.

I love you.

The words had been said using the Ouija Board, yet, he can almost hear them - he can almost see her lips moving, whispering those words, only for him to hear.

He closes his eyes. He feels closer to her this way. Could he really be falling for her? Is it possible to fall in love with a ghost, someone you can never touch or even see? But then, isn't falling in love more about the person on the inside rather than on the outside? What about people who fall in love with others who are disabled? Hell, look at at Stephen Hawkins! Two women totally in love with his mind. What about people who are born with physical disabilities? Many of them are still able to find love, someone out-there sees them for who they really are on the inside.

He remember a show on TV where this guy had such a horrible facial disfigurement that he would turn heads wherever he went. But he also recalls how someone he had met saw beyond his disfigured face and ended up not only loving but marrying him – she had seen what know-one else could – his soul. *Oh John. So you gonna marry her now? You gonna marry a damn ghost? Oh yea, nice one. And who are you going to invite at the wedding? Casper the friendly ghost and all his gang? Oh! And maybe you could also invite The Addams Family while you're there!*

Damn it, he hates that stupid inner voice! Always spoiling a good moment. And what makes it worse is that it always makes bloody sense. Why does it have to be right all the time? Well you know what? *Screw right and screw you! Yes, I'm falling in love with Lina and from what she said, very likely, she is also falling for me.*

John clenches his teeth, trying to control his mounting irrational burst of inner petulance. He starts to feel hot and kicks his quilt cover, letting it fall to the ground. He feels tired and really needs the rest but too many battles are being fought inside his head.

He needs to sleep or he won't be able to survive another week at work. He's been feeling like crap lately and it's going to catch-up with him sooner or later. Too many late nights thinking and worrying about Lina isn't doing him any good, not too mention the weariness he feels all over his body after the Ouija Board sessions. He feels like he's been pounding the macadam for twenty miles non-stop and his back muscles are so tense he could use them to string a guitar.

Sleep John, sleep.

OK. Counting sheep backwards from one-hundred seems to have worked in the past. Lets give that a shot.

He settles himself on his back, closes his eyes and starts seeing sheep jumping over a wooden, white fence.

100...99...98...97...

Lina's face appears in the middle of the meadow. He sighs. *Damn it!.*

Try again. 100...99...97...96...9-

He frowns. Did something just touch his arm? He opens

his eyes and looks down. Nothing. Maybe an insect? *Fuck it, need to sleep...*

He turns to his right side and closes his eyes again. *Right...*he'll get there eventually.

100...99...9-

His eyes open wide this time. He definitely felt something. Very light - like the wings of a butterfly. He keeps his eyes opened and stares at his right arm. Nothing. Maybe all this lack of sleep is really catching up with him – he's starting to feel things now.

He looks at the clock. 3:07 A.M. He picks up his quilt cover from the floor, tosses his warn out body to the opposite side of the room where the street-lamp isn't filtering through the thin curtains, sighs and closes his eyes.

Finally his body starts to sink deep into the mattress. His muscles start to relax and the heaviness of his exhausted soul welcomes the enveloping cocoon.

He can hear the rhythmic sound of his heart slowing down to a deep thud. He feels his limbs craving for the respite of his long days and his mind starts to sink into the abyss of reverie.

He senses something – like a finger slowly running down his arm. A furrow settles between his eyes. Is he dreaming already?

The furrow deepens. He knows he's not. The finger running down his arm is real. He is lying on his side and his mind is telling him that this is not a dream and that what he feels is real. He doesn't dare open his eyes. He doesn't want to make it disappear. He knows it's her...

"Lina?" he dares to whisper, hardly hearing it himself, not wanting to scare her.

The touch vanishes. He waits.

His lips form the words, but never leave his mouth. "Lina...please let it be you..."

Four fingers. He can feel them now, starting from the back of his hand. His eyes are still closed but if he were to open them, he is sure that she would there, lying right next to him, telling him that this has all been a bad dream. But he doesn't dare...

The fingers caress his arm, moving up towards his shoulder. The lightness of her touch tells him that she could vanish anytime if he were to move but a single muscle. He holds his

87

breath and all his concentration is focused on her ghostly touch.

He can feel every hair stand erect as her finger tips gently brush against the length of his arm. Goosebumps run through his body and he can almost see her, right here , right next to him. He wants to reach out to her and feel her the way he did that night. Part of him wants to believe that the last few days have just been a horrible nightmare and that the reality is right here, right now.

The fingers almost reach the top of his arm. They hesitate for a second, as if not wanting to break the touch, not just yet, as if wanting to relish the last few seconds of her solicitation for his embrace.

When her touch is gone, a vacuum envelops him like a torrent of emptiness pouring through his body. His eyes stay closed in the hope that her fingers might break through the veil of death and find their way to his world once again.

Sleeps finally takes hold of him, but just before it does, a soft murmur escapes his lips.

"Lina...I love you so much..."

But only darkness catches those words – or maybe not...

CHAPTER 17

Sunlight penetrates his bedroom and a playful ray finds its way though a small gap of the curtain. His eyes are still closed but the warmth of dawn caressing his face makes his eyes flutter open.

John feels disorientated for a moment but then it all comes back to him. His hand runs along his arms where hers had been the night before.

A shadow crosses his face as uncertainty tickles his mind. *Did last night really happen?*

He frowns. He is not so sure now. He knows that he had almost been asleep when he had felt her touch – or maybe he *had* already fallen asleep and hadn't been aware of it? If she did really touch him however, it would be so wonderful. He will need to ask her.

He lifts his arm and takes a whiff. His nostril flare in response to the vinegarish smell emanating from his armpit – *shower first.*

The water running down the base of his neck feels like heaven. The small headache that had started to develop slowly evaporates with the rising steam from the shower. John closes his eyes and can still almost feel her. His tries to recall the previous night - tries to re-live her touch. He wants so much for it to be real, but the inner doubt and reasoning tell him that it was just a dream – he will know soon enough.

He turns off the water and opens the shower curtain. The steam trapped inside the small bathroom keeps his body warm. He grabs the towel and rubs his body vigorously. His head feels a lot clearer and the thought of talking to her makes his heart gallop like a thoroughbred rounding the last corner of the Kentucky derby.

He grabs the brush sitting at the corner of the sink and looks up at the mirror. Then he sees it.

Just like before, written in droplets finding their way to the basin's edge, the ghostly letters – *her letters*.

TOUCHED U

The brush hits the tiled floor and brings him back to reality. All the doubts that have been pestering him since he woke up disappear at once, replaced by certainty – she really did touch him. His heart now reaches the end of the one and a quarter mile Derby, ready to leap out of his chest.

He picks up the brush, his hand shaking, and opens the bathroom door. The steam escapes and cold air creeps in, making him shiver at the sudden frigid intrusion. He wraps the towel around his shoulders before making his way to the bedroom.

He is dressed in two minutes and doesn't bother making his bed. He need her now...more than ever.

He switches the kettle on as he makes his way to the lounge and sets the Ouija Board on the carpet in front of the couch. He runs back to the kitchen, hits the dining table with his thigh – *mother fu....!* - grabs a glass and a coffee cup and fill them both to the rim with water and coffee.

With his finger now resting on the arrow that is sitting on the Ouija Board, he waits.

Nothing is happening. It's been five minutes and nothing...

John frowns and takes a sip of coffee. What's happening? He was sure that she would be jumping at the occasion of talking to him, especially since she has just acknowledged touching him the night before.

He touches his coffee cup. It's almost cold now. He looks up at the clock. Seventeen minutes. He's starting to worry. This doesn't make any sense. What's wrong? Could she be in trouble for talking to him? For...touching him?

His finger moves.

His heart misses a beat. "Lina? Babe is that you?"

He expects his finger to veer to the letter Y but it doesn't and instead slides, almost angrily, to the letter N and then O.

'NO'

He swallows hard. This is not good. "Who...who are you? Where is Lina?"

'SHE SHUD NOT TALK 2 U'

"Wa...why? It's not your goddamn business or anyone else's!" He knew this was coming, deep inside – he knew it. They, whoever *they* were, are not going to take Lina away from him. No, he won't let them! He feels an uncontrollable anger building up inside him.

"You!" he is yelling now. "You have no right to do this! This is between *me* and *her* and you have no right to stop us. Whoever the *fuck* you are!"

His finger suddenly presses down harder, making his fingernail turn white. Whoever or whatever this is seems pissed.

'SHE NOT ALOW N U NOT ALOW'

John takes a deep breath and tries to calm himself down. He must try to reason with this damned entity that's trying to separate them. "Well why? Tell me why. What are we doing that can be so wrong? We are not hurting anybody right? So why are you stopping us?"

'I NOT STOP I ADVISE'

John is taken aback. "What do you mean you advise? You mean you...can't stop us?"

'NO'

He takes a deep breath and the tension in his shoulders melts away. *He can't stop us – no one can.*

"OK...OK, let me get this straight. Are you saying that you can only advise us to not communicate but you cannot do anything to stop us?"

'Y'

John leans back on the couch and closes his eyes, making sure to leave his finger in place. A sense of relief envelops him. "OK. So what do you want? And where's Lina?"

'U AVE TO STOP'

"But why?"

'IT WRONG GOST N HUMAN TALK WRONG IN BIBLE'

John laughs out loud. "Bible? What the! You're asking me to stop because of the Bible? Buddy! I don't even read the Bible!"

'DANGEROUS'

He sighs. "Listen," he tries to reason. "No disrespect and nothing personal, but, whoever the hell you are, I don't really care. *And*, whatever the hell you want, I don't really care either."

His finger starts to move. He forces it back.

"Wait!" he interrupts. "I'm in control here. Not you! This is *my* body and you are only an intruder using it as a tool to talk to me. So don't you *dare* tell me what Lina and I can and cannot do. I don't know what danger you're talking about and honestly, I don't give a shit."

He let's the finger move this time. *See what the bastard has to say now...*

'WRONG DANGER BAD SPIRITS'

John starts to feel annoyed. There is no way that this...*thing* – whatever it is – is going to stop them from communicating. He takes a deep breath.

"Listen. This is the end of this conversation. I will lift my finger now and there is nothing you can do about it. *And*, the next time I put my finger on *this* board, I want it to be Lina on the other end and not you or anyone else. Understand?"

The finger starts to move but before it gets to the next letter, John lifts his hand and breaks contact.

He looks up in defiance.

"Never!" he shouts out to the empty air above. "Not *you* or *anyone else* will ever stop us from being together. So why don't you and all your spirit friends stick your ghostly finger where it fits and leave us alone!"

CHAPTER 18

"So why d'you ask me here for mate? I know you miss me, even though you bloody see me five days a week, but I'm pretty sure that this ain't the reason right?" He pauses for a second and nods. "Ahhhhhh! Got it! Lina right?"

James and John are sitting at Starbucks, both sipping on their Americano, black no sugar. It's Saturday morning and John couldn't wait until Monday to talk to James, especially after what happened this morning. Yes, a simple phone call could have done the trick but he'd rather have a face-to-face.

John takes a sip. "Well," he forces a tight smile and rubs the tiredness out of his eyes. "Nail on the head buddy. What else is there in my life that could make me desperate enough to see *your* ugly mug on a Saturday morning?"

James laughs. "Aahhh piss-off mate. You don't exactly look too crash hot yourself this morning and honestly, I'd rather be muff diving right now than sitting here with you."

John looks down and sighs.

James frowns and his smile disappears. He leans forward. "Sorry dude, must be important." He puts his hand on John's shoulder. "Come on, what's the matter mate?"

John looks up and sees the worried look on his friend's face. "OK. Well. Where to begin..."

"Try at the beginning," encourages James. "That's usually a good place."

"The beginning. Well OK. She...she touched me."

James frowns. "Touched you? Who?"

"Lina. I mean Lina. She touched me."

"Wha...what do you mean she touched you? I thought she's suppose to be...you know, well dead...a ghost."

"I mean," John says impatiently. "She touched me, on the arm, just when I was starting to fall asleep."

James looks at John with a concerned look covering his face. "Touched you? Wow! Like, physically?"

John wipes his mouth and looks around – no one near by. He leans forward. "*Yes*, physically. I was just about to fall asleep and I felt something touch my arm."

"Something?"

"Yes. Well like a finger at first, and then it was four fingers, running along my arms."

James scratches his head. "Dude! No way! You mean she actually like...touched you? Shit dude. But wait, hang on. You said you were almost asleep right? So, maybe you dreamed it?"

"No!" John replies defensively. "I mean it was real. At first I wasn't sure, but then when I had a shower this morning, she confirmed it."

"What do you mean, confirmed it?"

"OK, you know last time I told you she left a message on the mirror?"

James nodded. "You mean in the bathroom right?"

"Yes, in the bathroom. Well, after I woke up this morning, I was having a shower and was starting to doubt whether she really did touch me, or whether, as you said, I just dreamed it."

"OK...and?"

"Well, I didn't dream it, she confirmed it by leaving me a message on the steamed-up mirror.."

"Wow! What was it? I mean the message..."

John takes a sip of his coffee – luke warm. He grimaces. "Touched you. It said, touched you."

"Mate! This is seriously crazy. First you told me that she talked to you and now you are telling me that she actually touched you? This is serious shit dude. So...so what did you do? Like, after you saw the message? Didn't you like...freak out or something? Mate! I would've shit my pants!"

"Well, yea. I was pretty freaked out at first, but then, when I realized what she was saying...what she *confirmed*, I was ecstatic!"

James shakes his head, his eyes open wide in amazement and disbelief. "Man! That's crazy! Scary shit! I mean it's...fucking amazing!

"Yes," John agrees "But, that's not all..."

"What? You guys also had sex?" James smirks.

John sighs. "Please..."

James raises his hands in apology? "OK...OK, my bad, I'm sorry. Go on mate."

"OK. So then, as you can imagine, I was pretty freaked out but also pretty damned excited. Sooooo... I quickly got dressed and set up the Ouija Board. I put my finger on the arrow and was waiting for her, like a few minutes and I was wondering why she wasn't... you know, picking-up, and then my finger started to move. Expect...it wasn't her..."

A heavy-set man seats at the adjacent table and James gives the intruder an irritated side-way glance before leaning forward. He lowers his voice. "What do you mean it wasn't her?"

"I mean, it wasn't *her*, Lina. It was...well, I'm not sure but, some guardian angel or some shit. But anyway, he basically, assuming it was a *he*, asked me to stop."

"Stop what?"

"Talking. I mean, you know, communicating. He was saying that, what we are doing is wrong, and that ghosts and humans shouldn't be communicating."

"Wa...why not?"

"He said that it's against the bible and that it's dangerous."

"Dangerous? Why? How?" asked James.

"I don't know. I was pissed. I don't want to stop talking to her." he replies, rubbing the back of his neck. "I feel she needs me, like, she wants something from me," he lies, knowing that the truth is that he is falling in love with her. "So I basically told him to fuck-off and lifted my finger."

"Mmmmmmm," James says. "This is ama-zing...and bloody scary..

"Yea I know, it's crazy alright. Anyway, the reason I asked you out here is that, well, you are the only one I can talk to about this and I need to know what you think. The whole thing is nuts I know, but also I'm not sure what's happening. I'm not sure what she wants and I don't know now what *it* wants, I mean the other ghost."

James exhales and his mouth twists side-way in deep concentration. "Well," he finally says. "I personally reckon you, as that thing said, you should stop talking to her and go to the police."

John was looking for support from his friend and didn't expect this. "What? Seriou..."

James puts his hand up, stopping him. "Hang on mate, let me finish."

"OK...OK...sorry..."

"No worries mate. I mean, you didn't ask me out here at this ungodly hour on a Saturday morning for nothing, so you might as well hear what I have to say." He takes a sip of coffee. "To start with, the whole thing is so bloody crazy that I wouldn't even know where to start and the fact that a woman was killed and that you know about it and didn't go to the police is....well...I don't know...stupid."

"Yea, I know....but..."

"Wait, I haven't finished," James says impatiently. "The fact is that a woman was killed, and not only that, but you also know who did it, so this means that before you could even pull a booger outta your nose, the guy who did this could be rotting in jail. *And*, not only that, but honestly, what the hell are you doing mate? You are starting to fall in love with a..a ghost for god sake..."

"I...I'm not," John denies unconvincingly.

"Mate...don't take me for an idiot. It's bloody obvious and I'm not your best friend for nothing. Do you think I can't see what's going on?"

John swallows and looks down.

"I'm not tryin' to judge you or anything," continues James, his voice raising. "But don't you think this is getting ridiculous? I mean, come on...a ghost?"

John looks up.

"Guess you're right," he says sheepishly.

He has to lie. It's looks like even his best friend doesn't

support him now and that means he is on his on – he was hoping he wouldn't have to be. It's obvious now that no one will understand him – understand *them*.

James lowers his voice. "Mate, you know I'm always here for you, right? But honestly, you have to see what I see. How would you feel if it were the other way round? Think about it..."

"I know buddy, and you're right," John lies. He has no choice. He is tired and he doesn't want to argue. He knows deep inside that James *is* right but he knows also that he can't, or won't, stop himself. He knows how crazy this is but he can't help the way he feels inside. He can't help it anymore than a drunk can stop reaching for his next drink.

James pick up his coffee, looking a bit embarrassed. It looks like he regrets his harsh words but John knows that he is only trying to protect him.

"Hi..." John says. James looks over the rim of his coffee cup. "Hi, don't worry, I'll be OK. OK?"

James puts the cup down and smiles shamefaced. "Yea...I'm sorry mate. Didn't mean to raise my voice but, you know, you are my best friend and I'm really worried about you."

"It's cool, really. And don't worry, I've heard what you said and I won't contact her anymore," he lies again. "I realize how crazy this is." He gets up and looks at his watch – he doesn't want to be here anymore, he wants to be alone – or maybe, not *exactly* alone. "Tell, you what," he says. "Let me chew on it for a while and you'll be the first one to know what my next move is. Be it contacting the police or whatever. OK?"

James looks relieved and gets up. He puts an arm around his friend's shoulder as they walk out.

"Sure thing mate," he says. "And don't hesitate to call me anytime, anyplace, even-though you can really be a pain in the ass sometimes." he laughs.

John decides to walk home. He needs to think - his mind is filled with her.

"Lina," he whispers, knowing that only *she* can hear him. "I love you...I'll never let you go..."

97

CHAPTER 19

With his coffee and glass of water sitting next to him, John settles himself on the couch and sets the Ouija Board on his lap.

He hasn't stopped thinking about her on the way home. He also thought about what James had said – about how he should stop talking to her and how he should be calling the police. But he knows he can't. Well, he can, he can stop anytime, but the fact is...he doesn't want to.

He keeps thinking about how crazy the whole thing is. It almost seems like a movie, except it's not. He remembers a movie he saw called Ghost. *What was the name of the actors?* He remembers now. Patrick Swayze and Demi Moore....

He recalls the hot scene when she was making a clay pottery and Swayze came up behind her as a ghost and she could feel his hands on hers. He feels a twinge in his pants...

His finger moves. *Better not be that asshole.* He swallows. "Lina? Is that you?"

'Y'

A sense of relief rushes through his body. He thought that maybe they would stop her and that she wouldn't be able to talk to him again. "Oh Lina...I'm so glad. I was so worried after talking to that ghost who was asking me to stop talking to you. I don't know who the hell he was but there is no way that I'm going to stop. Are...are you OK? I mean they didn't do anything right? Like trying to stop you?"

'I OK NO WORY'

"I'm so glad to hear that," he exhales. "I couldn't stop worrying since the last time he came instead of you." he takes a deep breath, trying to slow down his racing heart. "Mmmmmm, is there a way that I can make sure that it's you every-time? Like, can I say or do something to make sure that *you* are the only one who can talk to me?"

'NO. FASTER ONE TALK'

John doesn't like that. So this means that the first spirit that gets hold of his finger will be the one he has to talk to – or not. Screw it, next time that asshole jumps in he'll just cut him off.

He takes the coffee mug with his left hand and brings it to his lips. He takes a sip and puts the cup back down. He closes his eyes for a second, trying to imagine her next to him - trying to feel closer to her. "Lina," he finally says. "I want you to know something. I've missed you...'

His finger moves. 'ME 2 MY DARLING'

John smiles at her response. This is not a movie, this is real – *she* is real. "And...I love it when you touched me. I could feel your fingers running up my arm. I didn't dare open my eyes in case it would break our connection. It was so...real, so wonderful. How did you do it? Are you able to do it again?"

'VERY HARD NOT SUR'

John feel a hint of disappointment. "Oh..."

His finger moves, cutting him off. 'BUT WIL TRY AGAN 2NITE'

"Oh babe, please try. I want to feel you so much..."

"ME 2 FEEL U FEEL ALIVE'

"Babe, I won't let him stop us OK? I won't listen to him. My friend James also asked me to stop, but I won't. I want to talk to you, I want to be with you, I want to feel you. Lina, what about you? Can they stop you? Can they hurt you?"

'NO'

"That means that they can't stop you at all from talking to me?" he asks, hopeful.

'NO JUST ASK CANT STOP'

"Oh Lina, that's great! That's means we are free. No one can stop us..." he thinks for a second. "But of course, there is no need to tell anyone right? Well for me anyways. I don't think I will tell James that we are still talking, I'll just pretend that we have stopped. He is my best friend and I know that he wants what's best for me but, he doesn't understand me, he doesn't understand *us*."

'AGREE NO TELL ANY1'

"Lina this is so exciting. You know, since...well since we met and this happened, I can't help but feel that this is my fault and..."

'JON NO'

John feels his heart skip a beat. He needs to get it to get it off his chest. He tries not to think about it but it's always there, at the edge of his mind – the guilt, the knowledge that if it hadn't been for him, she would still be alive today. "Wait, please, let me say what I need to say. The thing is that I cant help feeling that this is, well, at least partially my fault, since it was because of me that you stayed late that night and this caused him to go crazy and...well, you know..."

She cuts him off again. This time his finger presses down harder, making his finger-nail turn white as if to make a point. 'JON NOT U FAULT. HIS FAULT HE KILL ME. DESTINY'

John doesn't understand. "What do you mean destiny?" he tries to argue. "Being killed is not destiny! It's not faith! It's...it's murder. No one is *supposed* to die..."

'HE VIOLENT SOONER LATER DIE'

John feels his head spin. He can't believe what she is saying – how she's accepted her fate. "No, babe no! This is not right. This was never meant to happen. You were killed. You still had many years ahead of you and that...that bastard took your life away from you. Lina please, this is not *destiny*. Murder is not destiny..."

She relents. 'OK. BUT ALSO NOT U FAULT OK?"

John softens. "OK, I'm sorry. And I didn't mean to raise my voice. And maybe in a way you're right, maybe it really was inevitable. Maybe it would have happened eventually..."

'Y'

John takes a sip of water. His head has stopped spinning but he is still shaking. "Hey," he says. "Can I ask you something?"

'Y'

"What do I do? I mean...what do you want me to do?"

'NOTHING'

John is confused. "Nothing?" he asks. "You mean...you're going to let him get away with it?"

'N'

He rubs his face. "I don't understand. You don't want me to do anything and you don't want him to get away with it?"

'LATER'

'Later? Lina I really don't understand. What do you mean later?"

'LATER'

John sighs. "OK, I'm sorry. Maybe this is not the right time. Just let me know when you decide OK?"

'OK JON. NEED GO"

He is taken aback. "Is it something I said? I was just, you know, trying to help..."

'N'

He doesn't want to leave like that. "Errrrrr...will I see you tonight? I mean, you know, in bed? Can you try to...touch me? Like you did last time?"

'YES TRY'

He bites his lip, it's going to be a long day waiting for her. He wishes it were night time already. "I'm looking forward to it..."

"ME 2'

His finger starts to lift.

A surge of desperation rises inside him. "Lina? I...I love you..." he hesitates, not knowing whether it's too early, not knowing whether it' s right...

His finger comes back down.

'I LOVE U JON'

CHAPTER 20

It's been a long day, just as he expected. The seconds had become minutes and the minutes hours. He kept looking at his watch, counting the hours until he would be in bed with her – in a way.

If it had been up to him, he wouldn't have even left the house but would have gone straight to his bedroom after they had talked. But real-life shit had to get done and it doesn't get done by itself.

Finally he opens the front door. He would have a quick shower, a quick bite and hit the sack. He looks at the clock as he passes the lounge-room, 7:10 P.M – *well looks like an early night*. The day's been long and tiring, so why the hell not.

He half stumbles, half skips on one leg as he hurriedly removes his clothes, dis-guarding them higgledy-piggledy as he makes his way to the bathroom.

He turns on the tap, not bothering with the gas-heater to do its job, and swears as the cold water hits him. By the time the water eventually gets warm enough, he opens the curtain and hops out of the shower shivering.

Still wrapped in a towel, he heads straight for the kitchen. It's not that he really wants to waste time grabbing a bite but he knows that going to bed on an empty stomach means that he will have to get up in the middle of the night for a midnight snack, and well, he thinks, smirking, *who knows what could be happening at midnight...*

Half a packet of chips and a three-quarters of a banana later, his toothbrush finds itself laboring inside his mouth - not an easy task when a permanent grin is fixated upon it. He checks the small bathroom clock, 7:22 P.M. - *this could indeed be a new world-record.*

Without bothering with his PJ's, he hops into bed. A single sheet covers his nakedness and he notices the tent slowly rising in the middle of the bed. "Hang in there big boy," he whispers. He feels the sheet pushing against his manhood and closes his eyes.

He thinks of the night they spent together and the way she had mounted and ridden him. Slowly at first and then like a sudden tide, the intensity had risen to an almost unbearable rhythm. He remembers how he had tried to hold it, how he had wanted it to last for as long as he lived and if he had to die that day, he would have been totally happy to die in her arms and never look back....

A sudden sorrow feels his heart. He didn't die that day – but she did. He will never be able to hold her the way he did that night. They had only been together for a few hours and yet, he has never felt the way he did with anyone else. It's as if he had been blind and she had opened his heart to feelings he has never known existed – feelings that had been hiding in a place where continuance only resided before. Even now that she has moved on to another universe – a place of beyond, he cannot stop the way his heart leaps every-time he thinks of her and the sane part in him, that seems to be diminishing as time hemorrhages his remaining sanity, can do nothing but sit there and watch and try to reason with him and make him see how crazy his life has become. But he is beyond redemption now, beyond knowledge of what is real and what isn't. The line that separates fact from fiction, sanity from insanity, is becoming thinner by the day until one day it will all but disappear and his two lives will merge into one.

Just as reality and dream start to merge, he feels something – a touch? His eyes remain closed. He doesn't want to see the unseen. He wants to believe that she is there, sitting at the edge of his bed, her slender fingers running down the length of his arm.

He feels it again, something touching his finger tip, barely a sensation like a butterfly's wing. The touch is so light that he is not even sure whether it's really there or whether it's just his imagination wishing it.

His doubt vanishes when the slight pressure increases and her finger – he is almost sure of it now – makes its way along the inside of his own finger and settles midway down his palm. She starts to makes small circles inside his hand and a tinkling sensation that has the strength of an electric shock and the breath of a gentle breeze centers within his palm. He makes an involuntary fist and gasps at the thought of loosing her.

Her touch, brushed aside, vanishes for the slightest moment and starts again at the inside of his wrist. This time he can feel three fingers moving up his arm towards his inner elbow. Once there, he feels as if they hesitate for a while, as if wondering what to do next, before moving up to the base his neck. His shoulder moves up in an attempt to bring her fingers closer against his neck and feel her caress before she continues her phantom invasion.

He shutters as a thrill travels down his body when one of her finger reaches his ear and starts to caress its outer rim before finding its way inside. He's not sure but it feels that her finger is moist as if she has just licked it before probing and stimulating his ear.

He starts to feel aroused as his member pushes against the sheet and he closes his eyes tighter to fully emerge himself into her foreplay.

Her finger finally leaves his ear just as he thinks he can't take it anymore and this time he can feel them traveling down his face. On the way down, his lower lip is pulled down and he slightly opens his mouth, wanting to taste her once again.

One of her fingers enters his mouth. He tries to taste her, but there is only the sensation of her finger eagerly invading every corner of his mouth without any sense of taste, as if he were at the dentist and his mouth was numb. She swirls his tongue around her finger and all his senses converge into her probing member. He imagines her finger being her tongue and brings his head forward, wanting to feel more of her, and hungrily sucks on each of her finger in turn. He then opens his mouth wide, wanting her to push more fingers into it, which she obliges ardently.

His back arches as a tidal wave rushes down his body. His head turns from side to side, desperately seeking and feeling her hot, wet hand against his face and her hungry fingers pushing deep inside his mouth, hungry to explore every inch of his ravenous, gaping desire for her touch.

He has never known such vividness and such deprivation being fulfilled as their two beings merge in an embrace of taboo and subversion and as their bodies meet in a unison of intangible touch against all morals of sanity.

She continuous probing and pushing with   feverish intensity. After a minute, he cannot hold it any longer and explodes with such magnitude that he looses her and the world starts to drown in a swirl of his needs for her and her desires for him.

His drenched, exhausted body now lies in a pool of his own sweat and bodily fluid and as sleeps finds him, his last remaining thoughts never leave her...

CHAPTER 21

It's been a long day at work and he can't wait to get back home. With Lina constantly on his mind, the days at work have been so slow lately. She is like an itch, and the more you scratch it, the more it itches. He feels that his mind has been bitten by some giant mosquito.

As soon as he is home – it has almost become a routine now - he kicks off his shoes and under the time it would normally take him to think about what he would do tonight when things were still normal, he is showered and his stomach is full.

The Ouija Board is now sitting in front of him and his cup of water is at its usual place. The coffee, however, has been replaced by a nice Blue Label Johnny Walker he's been keeping for a special occasion, and after last night, how could anything be more special than their first time. The lights have been switched off and have been replaced by a thick, decorative, green and blue candle he's found at the market the week before. The small flame dances to the light night breeze that find its way through the open window and gives the room a phantasmagorical glow. John is ready for his date. He wants tonight to be special, he wants her to know how much she means to him.

As soon as his finger settles on the board, he can feel the slight pressure of Lina making contact and taking hold of it – well he hopes it's her anyway.

"Babe? Is that you? Sorry just want to make sure in ca..."

'Y'

His shoulders relax. The last thing he wants is to fall on that asshole who's trying to stop them. He looks around the room. With the candle light flickering, dimming the room into a shadowy, ghostly ambiance, he feels closer to her. He wonders whether she can also feel it – does she see, feel, the way he does?

He smiles. "Lina...I've missed you."

'ME 2'

"And I want to say that, well, last night was amazing. *You* were amazing..."

'TANK U. I FEEL SAME JON. I FEEL ALIVE'

John swallows. *Alive*. He makes her feel alive. He wants to know more. He wants to know how she feels, how she sees, *what* she feels... "Babe, can you tell me how it feels for you? I mean, for me it was amazing and with my eyes closed, I felt like you were there. Your fingers, your touch, it all felt so...so real."

'HARD TO SAY BUT TRY. I GHOST SO HAVE NO FISICAL BODY. WHEN WANT TOUCH U VERY HARD AND CONCENTRATE VERY HARD. I THINK FINGER, HAND, TOUCH'

John remembers and his hand instinctively goes to his lips – she felt so real. "What about you?" he wants to know. "How do *you* feel? I mean, can you feel anything like...pleasure? Like I do? Like...you did when we met?"

'IS DIFFERENT. I FEEL PLEASURE   THRU U BUT LIKE PULSE WAVE VIBRATION. THIS GIVE ME PLEASURE 2'

A furrow settles between his brows. He can't really understand, but yet, aren't human feelings similar in a way? A series of waves running up and down your body, sending each nerve ending on fire. An intense concentrated focus where pleasure is received.

"So you're saying that when your hand...or your...simulated hand was touching me, you also felt something similar to me?"

'YES I FEEL SAME LIKE U BUT DIFFERENT

MEDIUM. I FEEL U. SO I FEEL SAME. I FEEL THRU U'

John is mystified. This is not what he expected. So basically she feels what he feels – in a way. But what about when he gets an erection? Is it like...having sex with yourself? Nah...he doesn't want to think about it this way – too weird. "OK," he says, not really wanting to hear more details.

He looks at the time. Over an hour has gone past and they've barely said anything to each-other. The Ouija Board is good and it's doing its job but it's way to slow; there has to be a better way. He ponders for a moment and then it hits him.

"Babe, I was wondering. Well, since you can move my hand on the Ouija Board, do you think I can maybe hold a pen and, you know, you use my hand to write with it?"

'THINK SO'

"Great! Should we try? I mean, talking to you through the Ouija Board is great, but I think that when we have longer conversations, it just takes too long..."

'FOR ME OK'

John smiles. "Yea, yea, I know it's OK for you since there is no concept of time, but hey, remember that I have, and sometimes it really takes ages just to get a sentence out of you."

'OK TRY'

"Yes!" John says excitedly. "I'll let you go for a couple of minutes and quickly get a pen and pad and come back OK?"

'OK'

John lifts his hand and breaks the connection. He suddenly feels light headed as if he's just stepped off a treadmill. While he talks to her, there is no noticeable sensation but it looks like the whole conversations does take its toll. He wonders, whilst rushing to his bedroom, if there is a long term effect. *Well, don't think you'll find that one on Google John.*

He goes straight for his small desk and opens the drawer – a pen but no notepad. *Damn it!* He stands there like an idiot trying to think. *Pad, pad, pad...paper, paper...diary!* That's it! The diary that aunt Martha gave him for Christmas. He scratches he head. "Where did I put it?" he mumbles. He goes through the scene of coming home with the useless diary – guess his aunt forgot that people don't use these things anymore – and he sees himself looking at it and shoving it, unwrapped, into the drawer under the TV cabinet.

He picks up the pen, quickly makes his way back to the lounge room and opens the long drawer under the TV cabinet. A little black book, still wrapped in its transparent cover is sitting next to his shameful DVD collection. He picks it up and uses his teeth to tear at the packaging. *Why the hell do they make these dammed wrappers so freaking tough.*

Finally – no need for the Ouija Board now – hopefully. He settles himself at the dining table with the diary opened at the first page. He takes the pen in his left hand, just to make sure that his right hand – being right handed – doesn't interfere with her writing with some of his own thoughts. He knows, for a fact, that his left hand is as useless as an ashtray on a motorbike when it comes to holding a pen.

He puts the tip of the pen on the first page of the diary and waits.

Nothing happens. He feels it's been a long time but when he looks at the clock, it's only been a couple of minutes. He sighs – maybe it's not working and he should go back to the Ouija Board. Maybe one more minute, just one more...

The pen moves. It feels strange to see it move and see his hand moving with it, as if following it. He keeps the pressure on the pen but tries to keep it light enough for it to move freely. It proceeds downwards, forming a straight line and then to the right where it forms another straight line with a bar at the middle, followed by a 'S' shaped squiggle. His hand then lifts the pen, just enough to clear the paper, and comes down again half an inch to the right forming what looks like – if a two year old child were holding the pen - the letters 'm' and 'e'.

'Its me'

The writing is shaky, as if written by someone who has just broken his right arms and is trying to use his left hand, but he can make out what it says – what *she* is saying. "Wow! This is really working!" he exclaimed. "Babe! This is amazing! Why didn't I think of that before?" He pauses. "What about you? Is it harder? Same?...Easier?"

His hands starts moving again. John looks at the letters being formed. It's almost like someone is trying to write while holding his hand instead of the pen – it's clumsy but it works.

'Just a little harder for me, more concentration· But if better for you, for us, then I happy!'

John looks in amazement at the words she has written – *her* words, *her* handwriting. He is communicating with someone from another dimension, another world and all this time, all these stories and movies about ghost, making them seem like lost souls that are there to harm us, never realizing that they really are just *us* having simply moved on to another place – maybe even a better place. And now he feels so much closer to her. What's the difference really? People use words, emails, social-media to communicate. They meet online, fall in love, share things, sometimes across continents, without ever physically meeting. So really, he tries to justify to himself, what's the difference? Why can't he be falling in love with Lina? They are not hurting anyone, they have just found love where no one else has dared looking. They have made the impossible possible and he knows now, that nothing can stop them. They are bound by a love that no one can understand. He has found his soul-mate, across a universe – their intertwining universes, where even space and time cannot interfere. They have crossed a boundary where once death would do you apart, but not for them, not ever.

He feels his chest tighten with emotion and a single tear finds its way down his cheek, splashing softly on his lap and leaving a neat round circle on his boxer-shorts. He looks up, his tear-filled eyes make the room look blurry. He wipes his nose with the back of his hand.

"I'm sorry," he chokes with an awkward smile. "It's just that...this is so amazing, so wonderful. Last night was amazing and also *this* now. Everyday I feel closer to you. I don't know why, but since the day I met you, I knew you were the one. And even now that you are gone...to another place, that feeling doesn't want to go away. If anything, I feel it's even stronger now. I feel that maybe we were meant to meet before...you know. And...and...maybe destiny does exist...and...'

His hand suddenly moves, cutting him off.

'John, I know· I feel the same· I know one day he kill me· So many time he rise his hand to me and so many times I feel his fists and go in hospital with usual I hit door excuse, and nurses look me knowing not true· But I keep come back home because nowhere to go· He have my passport and he own me and I die like I know I will, in bathroom with my blood spill from his hands· But maybe you are right, maybe we suppose to meet night before I

die, and that why I come back you my sweet John, I also feel inside that you are the one and now I sure·'

The tears are now flowing freely and snot is streaming from his flared nostrils. John doesn't bother wiping them.. He cries for sadness and for happiness. The sadness of having lost her and the joy of having found her again. The mixed emotion makes his hands shake. He tightens his grip on the pen, he doesn't want to loose her, not now...not ever.

"Oh babe...I'm so sorry for what happened but also I'm so happy we have found each-other. It's all happened so fast but you mean so much to me already. I know that you are there and I'm here and it feels like a universe away, but I'm sure we can make it. Love conquers all my love. We have to keep trying to break the boundaries that are separating us and maybe one day, who knows, we can find a way to *really* be together again."

'I feel same my love· I think it fate that we meet before he kill me· I know since night together that we are linked· I not know how I know but I feel it, and when I die, I must to find you again· I know this can't be end· I on the other side but feel closer to you than anyone I know when I still alive· Maybe that what it take, ironic, but maybe I must to die for chance to be with you·'

John feels a lump in his throat. He takes a sip of whiskey trying to bring it down – the lump remains.

He takes a deep breath. He can feel his heart hammering in his chest. "Lina...babe, me too. I have never felt closer to anyone, and not just that first night we had together but also last night. It was amazing. *You* were amazing. I really don't know how you did it but it really felt like your hand was touching me. I felt as if you were right next to me, and even now when I close my eyes, I can still feel you. Oh babe...can you do that again?...tonight?"

'Yes· I also want touch you· I want remember be alive and feel love· My darling, I try even harder and try give you more· I want you be happy with me· I want you take me and love me like you do first night· My soul belong for you my darling· I love you'

John closes his eyes, remembering, feeling closer to the spirit of Lina than he has ever felt with anyone else alive. "Oh

111

my darling...I love you so much..."

CHAPTER 22

It didn't take long for John to get to bed. The moment they had stopped talking he quickly blew the candle, brushed his teeth; could she actually kiss him? he wondered - better be safe than sorry.

Now he is lying in bed, waiting. His eyes are closed and the traffic outside has died down to a lulling whisper – lucky his bedroom is at the back, away from the main street.

He tries to relax but he can't – something's wrong, he can feel it. It's been almost fifteen minutes now and she should have been here already. He knows that she was as eager to touch him as he was to feel her touch.

Something touches the back of his hand. He smiles. "Lina? Is that you?" he whispers, knowing fully well that it is her but wanting her acknowledgment with a gentle caress.

The touch suddenly changes and he feels a hand grip his wrist like a vice. He jumps and the hand lets go. "Lina?" a cold sweat suddenly covers his forehead.

'NO!'

John opens his eyes. He looks around, his eyes like marbles protruding from his head. He can smell the stench of his own fear. The voice. He didn't hear it – well he did, but it was inside his head. "Who...who are you?" he asks, his voice shaking.

'I TOLD YOU TO STOP!'

Yes, the voice is definitely coming from inside his head. No, not a voice. It's more like a thought, but it's not his thought. Something ...someone got into his head. "I...who are you? What do you want?"

'YOU KNOW ME. I HAVE WARNED YOU BEFORE. I HAVE ASKED YOU TO STOP COMMUNICATING WITH SPIRITS, BUT YOU DO NOT LISTEN.'

John licks his lips. He sits up, trying to feel less vulnerable. Sweat is pouring out of him like a river overflowing, soaking the sheets. How could this...this thing get inside his head? He wipes the sweat from his upper lip with the back of his hand.

Should he switch the lights on? He looks at the switch across the room. But that would mean getting out of bed. That would mean walking on the wooden floor where a hand would grab his ankle from under the bed – the same hand that has just grabbed his wrist. He suddenly feels like a kid again – like when he was five years old and had heard of the boogeyman lurking under the bed, waiting, waiting patiently until that one innocent child would have to leave the safety of his own bed to go to the bathroom. So many nights did he wet his bed, not daring to take the few steps it took to get to the bathroom, outweighing his mother's wrath against that hairy, filthy claw that would inevitably grab at his ankle should he dare taking that one, small, mortal step.

His fear is relived a thousand folds, but this time it's not a fairy-tale that was fabricated to scare little children – this time...it's real. And oh yes, of course he remembers who it is. It's that entity that was trying to stop him and Lina from being together, but he didn't expect *this*! He didn't expect *it* to touch him, to come into his damn head!

He takes a few deep breaths, trying to master up his courage. "Listen," he tries to sound confident even-tough he can hear the weakness and fear in his uncontrollable, shaking voice. "I...I told you b-before. Lina and I, we...we are not hurting anybody. I...I don't talk to anyone else OK? I don't *want* to talk to anyone else. So w-why don't you just leave us alone..." There is a, pleading, pathetic, desperate sob at the end.

'WHAT YOU'RE DOING IS WRONG AND IT IS DANGEROUS. *YOU* ARE GOING AGAINST THE

BIBLE, AGAINST GOD. LEVITICIUS 20:27. *HE* SAID THAT A MAN OR A WOMAN WHO IS A MEDIUM OR A NECROMANCER SHALL SURELY BE PUT TO DEATH. THEY SHALL BE STONED AND THEIR BLOOD SHALL BE UPON THEM.'

"But-"

'NO! YOU KNOW WHAT YOU ARE DOING IS WRONG. LINA IS WRONG AND YOU BOTH HAVE TO STOP NOW.'

John realizes that the voice in his head doesn't sound angry anymore. In fact it seems it's trying to reason with him – to make him see something he doesn't want to see. He tries to relax, tries to tell himself that the voice isn't here to harm him, maybe it's only there to warn him. "Who are you?" he manages to say, his voice now sounding stronger, more confident.

'I AM YOUR GUARDIAN ANGEL.'

"Guardian Angel?" John can't help but let a snort out. "Like seriously? *My* guardian Angel with like...with wings and shit?"

'YES.'

Now he is laughing. All his unwarranted fears have suddenly vaporized like mist on a sunrise "Oh come on! You expect me to believe that shit? *Come* on! This is all cartoons...movies! You know? The little devil and angel seating on your left and right shoulders, the good and the evil?"

'I AM WHAT I AM. EVERYONE HAS A GUARDIAN ANGEL AND *WE* ARE HERE TO GUIDE YOU. BUT GUIDE YOU IS ALL WE CAN DO. THE EVIL, AS YOU REFER TO IT IS *YOU*. YOUR EVIL THOUGHTS, YOUR WRONG DOINGS, YOUR DELIBERATE STAND AGAINST THE WORD. THIS IS ALL *YOU*. WE ARE HERE TO HELP YOU BUT IN THE END,' John hears a sigh. 'WE CANNOT STOP YOU."

He passes a hand on top of his head - it comes out wet. He looks around him . He will have to change his sheets. He swallows. He is calm now. He knows that this...guardian angel, or whatever it is, isn't here to hurt him, it just wants to warn him. But warn him about what? Lina and him love each-other. She is not an evil spirit that's trying to hurt him. She is Lina, the girl he met at the bar, the girl he made love to. She is the woman who has changed his life, who has made him feel what

115

he has never felt before - love. No. He won't give up on her, just like she didn't give up on him after she died. They are bound by love and no-one, from this realm or any other realm will be able to stop them – he won't let them.

"Hi..." he finally says, not knowing how much time has passed - not that it matters anyway. "You listen to *me* now. I know that you have your job to do and that maybe it's your job to help me., but honestly? I don't *need* your help and most importantly, I don't *want* you help, or anyone else's as a matter of fact. Lina and I love each-other and we are not going to stop communicating. If what we are doing is wrong, then so be it, and not *you* or anyone else, no matter what you say, will be able to stop us. What we have is pure, and maybe you can't understand that but Lina is the person I have fallen in love with right here, in this World, and it doesn't matter that she is there now, where you are coz the fact is, nothing has changed. She is Lina, she won't hurt me, she loves me and I love her, and nothing can stop us..." he let's out a breath, and holds out his chest in defiance. "Do you understand me? So *please...alone.*"

Nothing happens for a while. It seems the voice has given up. John looks up towards the ceiling – it's funny how you always look up when talking to ghosts – a minute ago he was under the bed - ironic. He looks around, looks at the light switch.

The voice comes back. It is calm now. It almost sounds pitiful, dispirited, like it has given up. 'MY JOB IS DONE JOHN. I HAVE WARNED YOU AND WHAT YOU DO FROM HERE ON END IS ALL ON YOU. I WILL NOT INTERFERE. I WILL STEP ASIDE AND LET YOU STRAY. YOU WILL SEE. YOU ARE PLAYING WITH FORCES YOU DON'T UNDERSTAND AND SO BE IT. GOODBYE JOHN."

A void suddenly feels his mind. He didn't realize the weight sitting inside his cranium until it is gone. He shakes his head to make sure he/it doesn't come back. He smiles, a determined smile. He feels strong now. He is not afraid anymore. He has stood up against the forces trying to stop them...for her – for their love. He can feel his heart pounding in his chest, but it isn't for fear anymore, it's for Lina.

CHAPTER 23

"**D**ude! I thought you told me you were gonna stop!"

John puts his coffee down and looks up at James sheepishly. "Yea, I know I did. I did say that. But...I don't know...it's stronger than me."

James shakes his head. "This is dangerous shit you're playing with mate..."

"Says who?" asks John.

James shrugs. "Hell, don't you watch movies? Like The Exorcise for example. And...and that ghost who came back last night and asked you to stop. Do you think *he* was playing with you?"

"It's not like that." John says defensively.

"It's not?" James' voice is rising. He looks around and lowers it. "He touched you mate! And then he even got inside your head. Just like the goddamn movie!"

John rubs his eyes. He hates this. He hates to go through this again but he has to tell someone, he has to tell James just to make sure he is not going crazy, cocooned in his own little world. "It's not what you think buddy. He wasn't trying to take over my body or anything like that. He was just trying to warn me..."

"Exactly!" cuts in James leaning forward. He licks the foam

117

from his cappuccino off his lips. "Warn you. Get it? And that means that they want you to stop. I mean come on...she is able to touch you and even *he* was able to grab your wrist without you *asking* for it."

John sighs. "No. I did ask. Well, I was asking her to...you know, touch me. And then he jumped in instead of her. So it wasn't like he just got inside my head without me asking for it..."

James raises his eyes to the ceiling. "Mate, do you know how crazy this sounds? You asked her to touch you? What, are you fucking crazy or something? We are talking about a bloody ghost here! A goddamn ghost mate! Why the hell would you ask a ghost to touch you?"

John looks down a his cup of coffee. He takes a sip, avoiding James's stare. "You wouldn't understand..." he mumbles.

"Try me..."

"I'm in love..."

Jame's eyes open wide in shock. He chocks on the last mouth-full of his cappuccino. "You *what?*"

John has had enough. He doesn't want to be judged. He's looking for support, not judgment. "You know what? Never mind," He starts to get up. "I think this was a mistake..."

James quickly grabs his shoulder and pushes him back down. "Mate, no please, I'm sorry OK? I just think that...the whole thing's bloody crazy. You've gone too far this time, and this is really getting out of hand. I mean, this isn't a game anymore, this is serious."

John wipes his mouth. "You don't understand. It's complicated. Nobody can understand what I'm going through...what *she's* going through. She came back for me, you get it? We met that night at the bar and it was amazing. And then after she died...she came back for *me.*"

"Yes, I do understand that that night was great and so on," James says, rubbing his neck. "But you need to get your head screwed back on dude. The wonderful girl you met that night is dead John....D,E,A,D, dead. She is not the girl you are talking to. The girl you are talking to is a ghost, not a girl mate, a ghost, a spirit with no body. Don't you see the difference?"

"No, she is not *just* a ghost. *She*, is Lina. *Lina*, the girl I met that night. She is the same person. And what's more, she also loves me, just like I love her. And I know..."

James recoils. "She *loves* you?"

John puts his hand up. "Wait, let me finish." James makes a show of zipping his mouth and nods. "OK, now listen," John continues. "Like I said, yes, she does love me and I feel the same about her." He frowns and thinks for a second. "And I'm totally aware of how crazy the whole thing sounds to you and maybe there is no way you will ever understand, but let me put it another way and maybe you will, at least, stop judging me..."

James puts his hands up. "Hey...sorry mate, just tryin' to help..."

John smiles, he didn't mean to be harsh. "I know, I know...it's just that...this has been very hard on me and I was hoping for some support that's all. And don't worry, I know you're worried about me, but it's just because you haven't been there, so it's hard for you," he shrugs. "Or anyone I guess, to remotely understand what's goin' on." He takes a sip of his coffee. It's cold. He grimaces and puts the cup back down. "But let me put it this way. You know...and it happens all the time in fact, that people always meet on the internet and fall in love right?"

"Mmmmhhhh."

"Right, and well really, what's the difference?"

"The difference is..."

"Wait. The fact is that they *do* fall in love. They meet, they talk for a while and eventually they find out that they match and then, it's inevitable...they fall in love."

Jame's mouth twists to one side and he nods. "Yes, I understand that. But the fact remains, and it doesn't matter how, that this is not someone on the internet that you're talking to and falling in love with. *This* is a ghost. And as you were told, not once but twice now, this is dangerous, and not to mention immoral."

John feels he's going nowhere. His friend is obviously not going to accept Lina or the fact that he is falling for her. He understands how James feels however, and he is pretty sure that if their roles were reversed, he would probably react the same way James is right now. "OK buddy," he sighs in resignation. "I can see your side of it and it's obvious that, no matter what I say, you can't see mine, and I'm sorry that I can't make you see it coz if I could, you would also see what I see. It's not all black and white anymore dude, it's like a whole new shade of grays have just materialized and I'm the only one who can see them. And who knows, is it really wrong what we are doing Lina and I? Is it really wrong for two people...two *beings,* to fall in love with one-other no matter where, who, or even *what* they are? Dude...she was human, she had a soul. In fact she *still* has a soul, a conscience, and...isn't that what makes us human?"

John is looking at James. He can see his friend is thinking about what he said – his mouth is twisted to one side as it usually is when he is pondering. James licks his lips and swallows before his mouth opens. "Mate...I can see what you are saying, and, as weird as the whole thing sounds, I think I can almost understand where you're coming from. Love can be really weird sometimes and hell...I've been in love, and sometimes with the craziest chicks out-there, the kind of girl you wouldn't want your parents to meet. So in a way, I know that love can make you do crazy shit." He pauses. "So you know what?" he smiles and puts his hand on John's arm. "You are my best friend...really, and just for that, I'm gonna go along with your craziness and I'm goin' to be there for you, OK?"

John feels his body relax. "OK..."

James lifts a finger in warning. "But! You must promise me that if any weird shit happens, like...that other crazy ghost, then you call me, day or night...*anytime* OK? *And*...you promise to be careful, OK?"

John smiles, looks at the time and gets up. "I will, I promise." He grabs the two empty paper cups. "Come on, guess we'd better get to work. Unfortunately, reality is calling..."

CHAPTER 24

The daily routine is pretty much down-pat now. Open front door, remove clothes on way to shower, soap-shampoo-rinse-dry, bedroom, slip on boxer shorts t-shirt, kitchen, quick bite – screw health – grab pen, notepad, settle down dining table, pen held, left hand seated lightly on paper.

John checks his watch - thirteen minutes – not that she gives a shit about time, but to him, time is precious and time spent with her even more so.

He feel anxious. What if it's him again? Well, he decides, if it is, he won't even bother talking to him and he'll just break off the connection and try again until he is able to contact her. He doesn't want to hear anymore shit about what is right or wrong and what he can or cannot do.

The pen moves...

'Don't worry my darling, it's me· Its your Lina·'

A sense of relief envelops him. He didn't realize the tension his body was in, like a champagne cork ready to pop, until he saw the letters of her message forming on paper. And he knew it was her in fact, as soon as the first letter had taken shape. He could feel no anger in the way his hand moved across the page - she doesn't press down on the pen the way the other ghost did. She is gentle, soft, and he even finds himself falling in love with the curls and shapes of the characters that she is forming through him as the pen slowly travels across the page. This is her, using him, working together, linked by an incomprehensible bond that enables them to reach out between their two worlds – her handwriting, even in its infantile peculiarity, is the most beautiful thing he has ever seen.

He let out a breath. "Oh my darling...I'm so happy it's you. I was really worried that..."

'I know·'

"You do?" He slaps his forehead. "Well of course you do!" he smiles. "How did you make sure that you were the one who grabbed the pen? You know, instead of him..."

'The fastest one get in first·'

John frowns. "Get in? I mean, I don't mind you, but that means that other ghost, the one who is trying to stop us, was also inside me?"

'No· Sorry no get in· I mean control·'

He sighs in relief. "Oh OK! So this means that he can't actually take over my body right? Like...the Exorcist?"

'The what?'

"The Exorcist, you know, the movie where this little girl gets possessed by a bad spirit..." Then John realizes. Of course she might not know., she's from Russia and maybe they don't even have that movie over-there. Not only that, but not everybody's into horror movies. "Sorry, maybe you don't know, silly me..." he pouts. "Well what I'm asking is that, is it possible for a ghost to take over my body, like totally, like I would have no more control over my own body."

'No not possible· Can only use you if let us· If decide you don't want then can't control you·'

He feels a lot better now, but still he doesn't like the idea that that last ghost, his supposed guardian angel, was able to touch him. "OK well, what about him? When he touched me."

'Yes can touch, but only short touch if you not want be touch· When I touch you, you want so I can touch longer· Also touch very hard for us so more easy we don't touch· But for you, I want touch, I want you happy, is very hard

my darling but want make you happy· And me also feel good, feel happy, feel human again·'

So that's it then, not really what his guardian angel was implying. There's no such thing as being possessed as it seems very difficult for them to even try to touch you for even a short time; and that's if he lets them in the first place. He takes a swig of his friend Johnny Walker – this is becoming a bad nightly habit – but hey, so what? Were he to die right now, at least he could be with her. A furrow forms between his eyebrows. "Babe? Can I asked you something?"

'Yes of course'

He takes a deep breath. It's not that he's in a hurry to get to the other side but he needs to know. "If I were tooooo...you know...die. Then..."

The pen pressed down hard and this time he feels it – anger. He swallows. *'John no! No! No!'* The writing has become furious, the pen almost making a hole in the paper.

"I'm sorry...I...I wasn't implying, I was just sayin..."

The pen starts moving again, faster this time, not giving him time to finish. *'John no· I love you but if u think dying, u NEVER see me again·'*

He is shocked - he didn't expect this. This is the first time he has made her angry and he feels like an ass. "Babe...I'm sorry, please. This is not what I meant at all...I was just asking. Of course I want to be with you but of course I don't want to die, well, not just yet anyway. Please don't be angry OK? I'm so sorry. Please believe me, this really is not what I meant..."

The pressure around the pen relaxes. He sees the color come back to his finger tips as blood rushes back in. His hand starts moving again, gentler, slower.

'No John· Please, is me sorry· I not want get angry· Is just I dead and no ready for this and now found you, not want be here babe, I want be alive· Want be with you·'

John feels a lump in his throat. He didn't realize what he was saying and didn't expect this kind of reaction from her. He now knows how she feels and that yes, she never did ask to be there - on the other side. Is anyone ever ready for this? Is there a right time for the inevitable? Maybe when you reach a ripe-old age and you have nothing more to give and spend your time reminiscing on all the things you could have done?

A time for regrets; a time to finally let go and move on.

He swallows and looks up, wondering where she is and whether she is looking down at him. "Oh darling, I'm so sorry that it had to be this way. I still can't help but feel that if you didn't meet me that night, you would still be alive today..."

'Yes maybe but this going to happen anyway· Inevitable· Maybe it happen earlier is better else cannot meet you· All has good and bad·'

"Yes, you're right. Maybe it really was inevitable and maybe we were really destined to meet that night...before he took your life."

John takes a sip of his whiskey. There is something troubling him - he needs to know what she wants. That bastard can't get away with what he did. "Babe, I want to ask you something. I want you to tell me what I'm suppose to do about your husband. He killed you and he can't get away with it. If no one knows, he will get away with murder. *Please*, I need this as much as you do, I can't let him get away with what he did...I..."

His hand starts moving, cutting him off. *'Babe no, no yet, I still thinking· I not want you to do anything yet· Please let me think and I let you know·'*

His mouth forms a thin line and he sighs. "But shouldn't I," he insists. "At least call the police? I mean who knows, maybe he will get rid of all the evidence including...your...your..." his emotions take over and he chokes on the next word. "body..."

'Please John no· Don't call police and my body not move, still there· He not dare move it yet·'

John gives in. "OK, OK, but as soon as you decide please let me know. I don't want him to get away with this. He needs to pay."

The pen presses harder into the paper, and this time it goes right through it. *'Don't worry my love, HE WILL PAY'*

CHAPTER 25

John is lying in bed, waiting. After they had finished their conversation, she had told him that she will try to meet him tonight and give more – he wonders how much more. She has asked him to close his eyes and pretend she is there, next to him. She wants him to remember the night they had met and she will try to make his dreams come true.

Now, lying here, his mind is split in two. He tries to focus on her and the night they spent together but another, more clouded side of him, is wondering what she meant by '*he will pay.*' He definitely felt her anger as the pen wrote the words in capital letters and the tip of the pen broke through the paper, leaving a permanent 'PAY' embedded on the soft wooden surface of the pine table. He's managed to remove the ink but the indent of the word remains. He is trying not too think about what she meant by that and what she is planning, but he can't. The anger he's felt and the capitalization of the word 'PAY' have shown her intent – she wants revenge, he is sure of it. But how...

He jumps. A touch. Her touch? He doesn't dare move. He closes his eyes tighter, trying to focus on the finger that is pressing lightly on his lower lip.

The finger slowly moves from the right corner of his lip to the left. He opens his mouth slightly wanting to feel more of her. He is sure now that's it is her – he can see her in his mind's eye - kneeling next to him, her finger caressing his lips, a mischievous smile covering her own.

The finger reaches the corner of his lip and goes into his mouth; not too deep, just playing with him, teasing him. He can now feel it slide sensually along his lower gum and his tongue reaches out to touch it. The finger stops moving and he feels it with the tip of his tongue. He focuses harder and can almost taste it – taste her.

He hears his own labored breathing and the drumming of his heart as his increasing heartbeat drives his desire for her. A tightness suddenly pushes against the single bed sheet as the sudden erection of his over-excited member makes itself known. He thrust his hips forward to meet the single sheet and imagines her pressing down on him.

A second finger joins the first. They go deeper into his opened mouth, and he pushes his head up, wanting to feel more of her and his hungry tongue reaching out for them. He starts to suck on them and they feel so real – so unimaginably real.

He feels a hand now, on his chest. This time it's not just fingers but her whole hand. The hand slowly makes its way down to his engorged member. John swallows, he is not sure how much more of this he will be able to take. The hand wraps itself around his shaft and starts stoking, slowly at first and then increasingly harder.

John thrust his hips up and down to meet her orgasmic rhythm. The other two fingers are now exploring deeper inside his mouth and playing with his tongue. John closes his lips around them and starts sucking harder. She lets him suck for a while and then pulls them out. She starts touching his face and toying with his ear. Her finger, still wet from his saliva, goes into his ear, not too deep, but just enough to drive him crazy.

His mind doesn't know where to focus anymore and everything becomes a blur. He can feel the heat rising as her hand strokes his erection faster and faster and his loins feel like fire. He turns his head towards the wet finger. He wants to suck it hard and wrap his tongue around it.

Her fingers finds their way back into his mouth. It almost feels like that unforgettable night as she plays with his tongue. He remembers her kiss, her smell and the scent and taste of her vulva. The memories are so strong that he can almost taste

126

her again.

Both her hands are now out of control. Touching, feeling, exploring. He doesn't know where to turn anymore, his head searching, seeking, right and left for a taste of her. His mind cannot keep up with the orgasmic stimulation that covers every inch of his body, and give rise to an unquenchable thirst. He knows now that his body has been deprived and that all his past sexual encounters have been nothing but a glimpse of the sensations his body is now trying, in vain, to embrace.

The rise and fall of each wave is one step closer to the tsunami that is as fatal as the drowning in the depth of his exaltation.

Her hands are everywhere now and his body thrashes in a tangle of sheets as his back arches towards the ceiling, every muscle trying not to cramp in an effort to meet the demands of his sexual fervor. His body starts to shake uncontrollably and his mind suddenly becomes powerless as the volcano that has been waiting for a thousand years erupts in an explosion of liquid fire leaving him in an exhausted heap, lying in his own ecstasy of sweat and seminal fluid.

His galloping heart starts to slow. If death were to come now, he would find comfort in it, knowing that nothing better could ever come out of his life, knowing that he has reached the edge of orgasmic insanity and that he will never want anything more in this life, or the next one   than her - his phantasm, his obsession..his Lina.

CHAPTER 26

Dawn filters through the curtain, sending a finger of early-morning light to his face. The ray dances happily, pestering his eye-lids to open up. He can feel the slight warmth of the sun dancing around his face, but he doesn't want to open his eyes – not just yet anyway. He wants to savor the moment. He wants to relive last night.

He vaguely remembers how it felt – how *she* felt. He knows that he has never known anything remotely close to this before. It was as if he had died and had gone to heaven, literally, and if heaven was this, then he would be happy to die over and over again. His thoughts try to congeal and form a clear picture of his memories of the previous night. He recalls her fingers, her hand. He remembers how they made him feel and the way they had touched him until...until he had totally lost it.

He squeezes his eyes tighter, trying to replay the sequence of events. There was something else – something more. It wasn't just her hands, it was like his whole body was locked into a spasm of elation. Her hands, her touch, her being were everywhere at once, like jolts of electricity. It was like a current running through his whole body, sending every nerve ending on fire. There was no pleasure-center and that's why his brain couldn't rationalize what was happening to him. It was something he had never experienced before and all his mind could do was to surrender, abandon him, and let him penetrate the fine line between pleasure and pain and the explosive climax that inescapably followed.

He opens his eyes, a smile painted on his face. He looks around the room. Expect for the sheet on the ground and the stains of his orgasm, there are no traces of her, not even a left-over scent. He recalls how after they had made love the first time, her scent had remained and he was able to hold the pillow to his face and smell her again.

The smile disappears and he feels a heaviness in his heart. *No John, there is no smell because she is was never really there now was she?* He shakes his head; he hates that voice inside his head because no matter how much he fights it, he knows it's always right. Could that inner voice be his guardian-angel trying to discouraged him? He clenches his jaw. "Fuck-off! I know it's you! And you're not gonna stop us! Get it? Now get the hell out of my head!"

Silence.

He sighs, pushes himself up on his elbows and checks his cell – 6:26 A.M. The alarm will go off in four minutes - he might as well get up. He needs to have a shower, he needs to get to work.

He swivels on his posterior and puts both feet on the bed-side rug, trying to snap-out of his reverie. *Come on John, you just had a great night! What the hell is wrong with you!* The smiles comes back. "Yea!" he shouts defiantly. He looks up. He knows she is there, looking down at him. "Good morning my love..." he whispers.

He stands up and heads for the bathroom – a hot shower and a black coffee is what he really needs right now.

***

John takes a sip of water and looks at the screen. His eyes can see the small Roman size 12 letters that form the Technical spec he's supposed to be working on, but his mind is in another world. He wants to talk her. He *needs* to talk to her.

He has a quick look around to make sure that no-one is approaching his desk, picks up a blank sheet of paper and puts it next to the printed Functional spec where no one can see it. He picks up a pen and lets its tip seat lightly on the paper.

It doesn't take long before letters quickly form into words.

'Hi babe'

John smiles. He loves it when she calls him babe. *'How are you honey?'* he thinks, knowing that she is able to read his mind and that he doesn't need to speak out loud. He only speaks out loud with her at home to fill in the silence, but he still hasn't gotten used to the idea of having a conversation inside his head - it doesn't feel normal. *Oh OK John...coz talking to a ghost feels normal right?* John sighs. *Just shut-up, will you? Keep your shit to yourself.*

'John, this not guardian-angel, it your subconscious'

He frowns. *'What?'* he can't understand. *'You mean that that voice that's always annoying me inside my head is not...him?'*

'No'

'But then, if not him and if only my subconscious, how does a guardian-angel guide you? Supposedly that's what he's suppose to do right?'

'Yes, but he not your subconscious, he your conscience. When see, do something, you feel right or wrong. He is the right but you decide you listen or not. He can't talk to u, he can only guide you but you decide.'

John rubs his tired eyes with his right hand. *'I see. So, that means that the voice inside my head is really just me?'* He considers. *'The annoying side of me?'* he muffles a laugh.

'Ha ha···yes!'

John looks at the last message. Was that a laugh? Wow! This is the first time she's actually laughed. "Babe," he whispers this time. "Did you just laugh?"

'Well, I message laugh but not really laugh. I know laugh when funny but can't really laugh. Just show you I happy and think u funny. HA HA HA!'

John can't help but laugh but it comes out too loud this time. He looks up guiltily and notices Gloria, the colleague sitting to his right, looking at him like he's just lost it – and maybe he has – if only she knew. He smiles at her and she looks down embarrassed.

"Babe," he continues, whispering. "That's wonderful. This is becoming more real everyday..." As soon as he says the word 'real', he regrets it, but there is no doubt she heard it.

130

"Lina...I'm sor..."

The pen moves before he finishes. *'John no· no need sorry· U right, I not real·'*

"Honey no!" he tries to apologize. "That's not what I meant, you know that..."

'John me ok· No worry· Me understand me not human· Me ghost but m'

John forces the pen to a stop. "Honey no! You listen to me," he compels, almost too loudly. "You *are* real OK? You are more real and more wonderful than anyone I've ever met and don't ever think otherwise. I don't care whether you are human or not, all I know is that I can't stop thinking about you and that when I'm with you, I can be myself. You know my every thought and every desire. You know how I feel and when I'm happy or sad."

He takes a sip of water and waits a few seconds. The pen doesn't move. He's worried that maybe he has upset her. What if she were to never come back again? He couldn't bear the thought of not having her in his life, not now...not after all this. "Babe please, you know how much you mean to me. I know you can feel it with every beat of my heart that beats for you, and I know you can hear it with every thought in my head that whispers your name. Honey...I know you know...please forgive me..."

He feels the pen hesitate. She is still here. She hasn't given up on him. His hand is shaking; he is not sure if it's him or her...or maybe both. He didn't realize how much she really means to him until the thought of losing her has crossed his mind.

Finally her words reappear on the page. The pen is still shaking, but this time he knows it's not him. *'John, I understand and I can't live without u too· If ghosts have tears I cry now· I cry of happy· I cry because found you· I cry because love u· I cry because u make me feel···'* the pen wavers, just for a second. *'···real· Thank u my love·'*

A knot forms in his throat and his chest feels like a vice is trying to squeeze the life out of it. A single tear escapes and flows down his face before landing on the paper and spreading the last word 'love' into the shape of a heart. His fingers open and the pen drops silently onto the carpet.

John knows now, he can't live without her – not now...not ever.

CHAPTER 27

Again the day's been too long. Every hour he spends without her is a reminder of how much he misses her and how much she means to him. She fills his mind, every minute of every day.

He didn't get much done today. He kept going over what she had said about him making her feel real and that if she could cry she would. What must it be like, he wonders. What's it like to be a ghost, to have no physical body, just a soul, a thought floating around endlessly with no sense of time and space. What's it like to want to feel real, to *be* real, and not being able to. She wasn't ready for this, not now, not like this. She was too young to die in the hands of a battering pig.

And now she's gone but she has found him. John knows this is crazy. Damn! His inner-voice told him often enough. But who wants to listen to sanity anyway? This world is full of insanity anyhow, so what's point of being rational? And who makes the rules anyway? What's right and what's wrong? Live and let live...yea...that's right.

His head suddenly drops and he jumps up almost falling off the chair. The pen is still in his hand – thank God for that. Why is she taking so long? He looks at the clock, almost thirty minutes. Something must be wrong. He feels a knot in his stomach. He has a bugging feeling that maybe he really did upset her when he mentioned the word real. What if...

The pen starts to write. He tenses, almost dropping it – what if it's not her?

'Hi babe· Don't worry is me'

He let's out the breath he's been holding. "Oh darling, I was so worried. I kept thinking that maybe you wouldn't come back..."

'I here no worry· I do something so not come straight away· Sorry u worry'

John feels like an idiot. Maybe he is being a little too melodramatic - worrying all the time. He should know by now how she feels about him as he feels the same about her. He shouldn't be having any doubts about whether she might show up or not.

"I'm sorry for worrying so much," he says. It's just that, you mean so much me and...I don't want to loose you."

'I feel same my darling· You no need worry, I will always come back· Sorry took long time·'

"No, no...please don't apologizes, it's OK, really. Like I said, I tend to over-think sometimes." He picks up his whiskey and takes a long swig. He winces and closes one eye – he forgot that the new bottle he's picked up on the way home is 5 degrees stronger. The aroma fills his nostrils and he feels the golden liquid slowly descend to the pit of stomach. He closes his eyes and enjoys the warm sensation and the slight lightheadedness that follows.

He opens his eyes and frowns – something she said. "Mmmmmm, babe? You said you were busy...what does that mean? Are there, you know, things to do up there?" He can't even start to imagine.

'Sorry yes· Busy· I was checking husband'

He can't understand. Why would she check on her husband? "Honey why? Why would you do that?" he asks with a pang of jealousy.

The pens hesitates for a second. John doesn't like this. He remembers the last time the pen did that – this can't be good.

Finally it starts moving. *'John I need ask you something'*

He swallows. "Yea sure babe..." he says. But he is not really sure now.

The pen moves again, more urgently this time. *'U love me?'*

He looks up at the ceiling and let's out a breath. So that was it? "Babe!' he says. "Honey, of course I love you! Doesn't it show? I mean you can read my mind right? So you should know how I feel even without asking..."

'I know my love and I also love u more than anything'

He wonders where this is going. She was late. She was checking on her husband. And now she asks him if he loves her. "Honey, what's wrong? Why are you asking me that?" He starts to feel uneasy and shifts on his chair. A bead of sweat forms high up on his forehead.

She continues. *'John· I need ask u do something· Not know how ask'*

He clears his throat. "Babe, just ask, it's OK. You can ask me anything...really."

'U sure?'

"*Yes*, I'm sure" he replies, noticing the impatient tone in his voice and hating himself for it.

'OK· Need u do something for me· Need you help'

OK,OK, this can't be that bad. Maybe she needs him to get something or maybe...tell the cops? "Hey...I love you, remember? Whatever it is, you can ask me. I promise I'll help OK?"

The pens hesitates again as if she is not sure she wants to continue. Then she does. *'I want u kill him'*

John's eyes open wide in shock. He stares at the word *kill*, as if it just bit him and spread its poison. His mouth opens, but nothing comes out. His head starts to spin and he notices his hand shaking – or is it hers. When the words finally reach his lips, he can hear the shaking in his own voice. "You...you want me to...what?"

This time, there is no hesitation and he feels her anger again - he feels the pen pressing down on the paper. 'KILL MY HUSBAND'

He takes a deep breath. He expected anything but that. "Babe, do you know what you're asking me to do? I mean..."

'Yes· John, please, I know this hard and - '

He stops the pen. " Hard? What you are asking me to do is

not *hard* babe, it's crazy!" he shakes his head - he can't believe this can be happening. "Lina! You are asking me to kill a human being! Someone I don't even know. Someone who has done nothing to me..."

This time his hand goes against his will, almost as if her anger makes her stronger. *'Someone who kill me. SOMEONE who stop me from living.'* There is a pause, as if she thinking of what to say next. The pen moves again, it's shaking. *'You said u love me John.'*

He swallows. He feels like an asshole, but how can she be asking him that? How can she ask him to kill somebody. He is not a killer for God sake! Sure he wishes he could kill his boss sometimes, but that doesn't mean he *really* wants to kill her. God, he can't even start to imagine what it must feel like to kill someone.

He needs to reason with her. There is no way he can do this. "Babe, please...you don't know what you're asking. I mean, this is a matter for the police. Can't I just go to the police? And then they can investigate, you know, and put him behind bars...where he belongs. This is the twentieth century honey and you can't just take the law into your own hands. You can't just go and...kill someone."

'John, he kill me. He take my life. He must die for what he do to me. I have life, I not ready for this, and now I dead. I must do to him what he do to me.'

"But..."

'John, please. I love u. Please, for me.'

He looks down at his hand, at the writing – her writing. Lina...*his* Lina. He clenches his jaw. This is wrong, it's so wrong, but he knows deep inside, that it's right. He can hear his heart pounding as blood rushes into his ears. He doesn't want to loose her. He knows that he is all she has now and he also he knows that she is the most important in his life.

A cold sweat travels through his body, making his shiver. He knows he will do it. The voice inside tells him that's it's wrong, but he knows that the love he has for her has no boundaries. - no right or wrong. He is fighting a loosing battle, and he knows that he will loose and fight - fight for her. Fight for the life that bastard has taken away from her.

He stares at the wall in front of him. His eyed narrow into

two narrow slits – focusing on the inevitable. The fatal words come out through clenched teeth. "Babe...I love you. I'll do anything for you...I'll kill him for you..."

CHAPTER 28

The thought of having to kill someone keeps running through his head, making him feel nauseous. How can he kill anyone? He shouldn't have said yes so fast. He should have told her that he needed to think about it.

A picture of him with a knife being driven into some fat guy keeps running through his mind. It's the kind of thing that you see in movies and yea, it's fine in movies when it's all fake and then the guy gets up two minutes later to go and have a shower to wash off the ketchup, but this is real – the blood will be real. He's heard that blood has a metallic smell and he can imagine her husband's blood running through his fingers as it spills out of the hole in his guts – no, his neck...

John shakes his head. He needs to talk to someone. He looks at his phone. James? No, there is no one – who the fuck do you talk to about killing someone? He's on his own...

Why did he say yes?

He needs to to talk to her. He looks above the cubicle wall and no-one is coming towards his desk; they are all working their asses off. They think that their life is complicated because their project is due tomorrow...shit, they have no idea what complicated *really* is – just try falling in love with a ghost who's just asked you to kill her husband.

He grabs a piece of paper and pen – he needs to try to

reason with her. He holds the pen above the paper.

It's been over ten minutes and the pen hasn't moved – he can't feel her presence, but he knows she's there. "Come on babe," he whispers. "Please, I really need to talk to you..."

Nothing.

Oh yes, she knows what you want alright, she can read you mind, remember John? So what do you think she will do? Pick up so that you can try to talk her out of it? Come on John...be a man! That asshole killed her...and you didn't even protect her...

Not that damned inner voice again – why is it always against him? "Protect her?" he whispers angrily to himself. "How the hell was I suppose to protect her and how the hell was I suppose to know he was going to kill her?"

Oh come on John...don't be a pussy. She told you he was beating her up, so what do you think was gonna happen?

"Yes but..."

Always 'buts' with you ain't it John? The man with all the excuses and no balls to back him up. He killed her John! All she is asking from you is to show her how much she means to you...how much you love her...

John feels the sweat building up in his right armpit and staining his shirt – the musky odor reaches his nostrils and they flare in disgust at his cowardice. Why is that damned inner voice always fucking right. He takes a deep breath.

"Damn it!" he says, almost too loud. "Damn you! Shit! Fine! I'll do it OK? I'll do it! Just...just leave me alone!"

He tries to calm down. He takes deep breaths and tries to slow down the heavy breathing that makes his chest heave up and down. He looks at the pen; his hand is shaking.

He puts the pen down.

There is no need to talk to her now, he will do it. He *has* to do it. No more hesitation, no more going back. He will talk to her tonight, he will need her. They will plan it together. He will do it...for her...for their love...

CHAPTER 29

John takes a sip of Johnny Walker and tries to calm himself down. All day, the recurring thoughts of what he is about to do have been haunting him non-stop.

He looks at his hand. In it is the pen that is his communicative tool with his ghost lover. Sometimes he thinks about the two of them and that's when he realizes how crazy the whole thing is; but then love it crazy, isn't it? So why not? Why not be in love with a ghost and...why not take revenge for her? Would he take revenge for her if she were alive and her husband had hit her? Yes. He knows he would. Maybe not kill him but definitely beat the shit out of him.

So what now? That asshole didn't just hit her, he killed her. An eye for an eye. He deserves what he's got coming to him. *See if you like having your life cut short...asshole.*

Before the pen even starts moving he can feel her, like a very weak current running from his shoulder down to his hand. Then the pen meets the ruled piece of paper that is sitting on the lounge table and the words begin to take shape in her child-like scribble.

'Hi babe· Its me'

He smiles and the tension leaves his shoulders. "I know," he says. "I felt you even before you started writing. It's amazing..."

'John· Thank you'

He frowns. "For what?"

'For do this for me'

Of course, she would know. She has probably been reading his mind all afternoon and she already knows that he's decided to do it. This is something he will really have to get use to – no secrets from her.

A smirk crosses his face. "Ha well, so I guess you already know right?" He imagines her having a knowing smirk of her own.

'Of course ha ha' The pen stops for a second before continuing. *"But also I want u know I feel bad· I know you no want do this but u need understand why'*

John shakes his head. "Babe, I do understand why. And even though I do think it's crazy, I get where you're coming from..."

'Come from? Dont underst-'

John sighs – language barrier. "No, I mean that I understand why you want this...why you *need* this, and," his mouth twitches to one side. "Even if the whole idea scares the shit out of me, I'll do it for you...for us."

That's it, done. Committed. And somehow, now that the decision has been made, it doesn't feel that bad. In fact, it almost feels...right. "Honey," he says. "What I'm going to do is very dangerous. It needs to be planned *and* it needs to be done right or I could end up in jail for a very, *very* long time..."

'I will help'

"How? How can you help?"

'I know all· I can know where he is all time'

John scratches his head, a deep farrow forms between his eyes. "Mmmmm yes, I see," he says. "Well, since you know where he is all the time then it would be easy enough for me to be there at the right time and place..."

'Yes'

He scratches the subtle growth on his chin and ponders for a moment. "I think the best thing to do is to make it look like a robbery gone wrong, this way they won't be looking for a real motive, just a robbery."

'Agree'

"Does he drink? You know, like go to the bar for a drink occasionally? I know Russian man normally like to drink vodka right?"

'Yes he go bar friday nights after he do work'

"Right. We may be onto something here. Mmmmmm....where is the bar? Is it in a quiet area or in the city?"

'Is not far from home so he walk when drink too many'

John squints and take a mouthful of whiskey, twirling it around his mouth before swallowing. He feels the gratifying burn as it descends to his stomach and a slight numbness follows. "OK, OK, so how far is home and does he take any alleys or just the main roads?"

'Sorry dont understand alize'

John sighs. "No, its *alleys*. Alleys are small, dark streets between buildings and cars usually can't go there...it would be a perfect place away from prying eyes."

'OK, understand· Yes, after drink, way home have alley behind bar· Is dark and smell'

This is perfect. John can already see it in his mind's eye – just like a movie. Her husband, half drunk and staggering into the dark alley. He is waiting behind an industrial bin, knife in hand. Her husband approaches, he has no idea he is about to die, then he gets near the bin. John jumps in front of him and stick the sharp blade into his fat gut. Her husband crumbles to the ground and ends up lying in a paddle of his own blood gushing out of the opened wound. John walks off, leaving him to die.

"Babe? I think we can do this, but I will need your help..."

The pen doesn't hesitate and he can feel the pressure increase on the paper. *'Babe, anything I can do I will do'*

John bites his lower lip. "OK. We will do it this Friday night. I don't want to wait too long or I'll loose my nerves." He closes his eyes, generating a plan in his mind. "First, you will tell me where that dark alley is, then on Friday night, I will be waiting in the car nearby. In the meantime, you will keep an eye on him and once he's about to come out of the bar, you'll let me know. I'll make my way on foot into the alley and wait for him there. Then, when he comes, I'll...kill him."

The pen is shaking, only slightly, but he can feel it. He's not sure if it's her, or him, or maybe both. *'My darling· I do this· I tell you all· I know I ask a lot of u and I know hard for u to do and I love u so much for do this for me'*

John swallows. He downs the rest of his whiskey, releasing the lump that has been forming in his throat. "Babe, yes you're right. This is hard for me and my conscious keeps telling me how crazy this is and that I shouldn't even be considering it. But there is something more powerful than right and wrong my love...and it's you, and what you've given me. So this is the one thing I can do for you. *This,* is the one thing that it right."

Later that night, John is lying in bed. His eyes are closed. He feels her hand running down his his chest., caressing him, exploring every inch of his body and fulfilling every concupiscence of his desperate outcry . The orgasm that follows is more intense than anything he has ever known. Eventually, sleep takes over and he dreams of her, in his arms, making love like the very first time...

CHAPTER 30

The car is dark inside. He decided to park it away from the street lights to make sure that any passer-by wouldn't be able to see him seating there. His eyes are peeled and focused on the alley's street corner. His left hand is resting on his thigh, waiting for her signal – her lifting his index finger three times would tell him that her husband has left the bar and that it is safe for him to go ahead; two means abort.

He takes sip of whiskey. He knew that he would have the jitters and the whiskey would help to take the edge off. He was right. His right hand, which is grabbing the steering wheel too tight, is shaking like crazy, and he can't stop it. He takes another swig.

He looks at the luminous digital clock on the dashboard. It's been forty minutes. He feels like a school kid waiting for his exam to start – and he didn't study. The butterflies in his stomach keep telling him that you can never be ready for something like that, and that he will fail.

Suddenly his index finger rises – it's the signal. It goes down once, twice and then...there is hesitation. His finger is up in the air and not coming down – maybe she's changed her mind. The few seconds feel like an eternity. He feels a bead of sweat running down his temple. And then the inevitable happens - three.

The street is as dark as deep space and the moon is barely shining; only a small sliver helps him to discern the shape retreating ahead of him. The adrenaline starts to kick in and he feels his heart accelerating.

As softly as moonlight steals the skies, he follows his prey, getting closer with every stride. The man swerved into the dark alley. The hunt is on. His body tunes in to the task ahead and his primal predatory nature takes over. He can feel the blood rushing through his veins and every heartbeat is like a drum inside him. His eyes, like the eyes of a cat, can now see every detail and his senses become as sharp as an eagle. Every step is a step closer to the inevitable. He can already visualize the impending death that is to follow.

With his eyes fixated upon his prey, his hand slowly glides down the length of his body in search of the blade that is to achieve the deed. The handle feels good in his hand and the cold of steel against his palm brings shivers down his spine. The power of the weapon makes him feel like a God – tonight, he decides who lives and who dies.

Now closer, like a hunter closing in on an unsuspecting gazelle, his animal instincts materialize He clenches his jaws, determined, and remembers Lina. *You will die and you will burn in hell, and you will rot, you filthy scum. I hope you suffer through eternity and that the pain tears your apart as you have torn her from this this life. You have taken her life and i will annihilate you, even if it means we are bound in hell together...*

He is only inches away now, every step a step closer to destiny. He can now hear her husband's breathing - his last breath. He tightens his grip. The blade in his hand feels like an extension of him – an extension of her. Closer now, almost there.

He frowns. Something's amiss. He can suddenly feel her, it's not his hand any-longer – *she*'s in control. The hand comes up, the blade catching the moonlight for one brief moment and the other hand – *his own hand* - comes around in an arc as swift and silent as an eagle, and lands tightly around her husband's mouth, making sure that no cry can escape. Her hand, the one with the knife, quickly goes around the other side and sinks the blade deeply below the left ear. Then, tearing at the flesh, severing sinuses and muscles, it comes around to the right ear effortlessly as if through butter, opening a wide gash, which at first almost looked like a wide grin, until blood starts to ejaculate in a torrent.

The blood is now flowing between his fingers. It feels strangely warm and the macabre embrace almost feels like a mother holding her child before sleep releases him from wakefulness . There is hardly a struggle as the body is slowly disengaged from the fragile tenacity of life and melts into his arms like snow on the first Spring day. It crumbles slowly to the pavement and lays there motionless. The torrent, that was once, is now but a trickle - a stream leaving its bodily constraints. It is done...

John looks at his hands, sticky and wet, and the strange smell of iron feels his nostrils. He glances around nervously - no one...he has to hurry. He reaches into the back pocket of the dead man, careful not to step on the blood that it now creating a large pool around the body, and pulls out his wallet – it has to look like a robbery gone wrong. He peers inside and pulls out all the bills, not bothering with the small change. He is almost tempted to check the man's id but he knows it will haunt him; he'd rather not know. He pockets the cash and throws down the wallet – it lends next to his face. John can see one eye; it's still open. He knows he's dead but that eye, staring at him, seems to have a million questions for him.

John doesn't bother to reply. He turns back the way he

came and in a state of numbness, he fumbles for his keys, opens the car door and leaves the corpse among the garbage in the alley – exactly where it belongs.

CHAPTER 31

The bathroom is steamed-up. The fan is still not working and fixing it's been the furthest thing from his mind. He's been standing in the shower for over half an hour. He has soaped and re-soaped but you can't wash away fear and guilt.

The scene keeps playing in his mind. He remembers how impossibly wide that gash in his neck had been and how much blood had poured out from it – it seems impossible that there can be so much blood in a human being.

He doesn't know how he can live with himself after what he's done. No. What *they* have done, Lina and him.

It wasn't his hand that severed the sinuses and windpipe in one smooth motion, he knows it – he felt it, it was hers. *Don't kid yourself John...you know it was you...it was your hand, your intent, it was you.* He shakes his head. "No, no, no! *We* did it! Me and her...we did it! And I don't care what you say, he deserved it!" he wipes his face, he needs to get a hold of himself.

The water is getting cold. He shivers and steps out of the shower. He wraps a towel around his waist and heads for the bedroom. He dresses quickly and his feet automatically carry him to the kitchen.

The coffee is made and the pen in his hand and paper on the table are waiting. He needs to talk to her – it doesn't take long.

'Hi its me'

John swallows. Damn lump...it seems to be permanently there the last few days. "Hi..." he chokes. "I...I did it babe. I...*we* did it..."

'Yes honey· WE did it· I not want u feel bad· I use you hand· I kill him'

John feels bad. What she just said, even though he knew it already, makes him feel like he didn't have the guts to do it himself and she was obliged to give him 'a hand'. She was there just when he was about to cut him. *She* did the deed and she's just admitted to it. "Babe I'm sorry...it...it should have been me and..."

He doesn't have time to finish. *'No please John· NO· You already help me and u were going to do, I just come at end when kill him'*

John frowns. "You mean you intended to use my hand to kill him ?"

'Yes I want do that· I kill him no u· ok? U just help me'

So this was part of her plan. She brought him there so that she would be able to take her revenge. She found a way to get back at her husband for what he did to her – an eye for an eye.

Now he wonders. "Babe, can I ask you something?"

'No John I no use u· I LOVE U'

Damn...he can't get used to her reading his mind before he even has the chance to verbalize his thoughts. "Right! Got me there!" he chuckles. "You're one step ahead of me...again."

He imagines her smiling, her beautiful smile – god he misses that.

The pen presses down as if to start writing but instead it forms a semicolon, John frowns, and then a dash and a closed-bracket... ' :-) ' a smiley.

John explodes into laughter and the tension he's been feeling suddenly vanishes. It will be OK, he knows it will. He loves the way she expresses herself. She is so...human. He winces – not a good thought – and he knows that she *heard* that.

'Is good see you laugh· I was worry about u'

"Oh babe, I'm OK. Well, I wasn't...before we met you

know...but now, I'm OK, because of you honey. And...I want you to know that *yes*, what we did is wrong in the eyes of...well, whoever, but another part of this feels right. We did what had to be done. I just hope now that it will just be front-page news for a day or two and that within a week all will be forgotten. Eventually, they will find where he lives and they will find your...well you know. Anyway, I don't think they can link me to this, I basically don't exist.'

'What about James?'

"James..." he almost forgot about his friend. "Well, he does know about you and when he hears that your husband was killed in what looks like a robbery, I don't think he'll put one and one together. And...well even if he does, I'll tell him that he's crazy to even think I could kill someone, which of course he knows I wouldn't be able to. I mean this stuff only happens in movies right? It'll be OK my darling, don't worry."

' :-) '

John smiles. He feels his heart pounding. He takes a sip of coffee. He's almost glad now that he was able to do something for her. For some reason, it doesn't feel as bad as he thought he would. Maybe it wasn't the right thing to do, but honestly, one less scumbag on this earth. Men who beat women are nothing but low-life pieces of shit and deserve what they've got coming to them. Killing him might have been a bit drastic, but oh well...he shakes his head, losers can't be choosers.

"Honey, I feel better after talking to you. After coming home, I felt horrible about what I did and it felt like no matter how many showers I took, it could never wash off the guilt and the knot that had formed in my stomach."

'I sorry I made u do and feel guilt'

He shakes his head. "No please, don't. It was my decision and I agreed to it." He sighs. "Babe, why don't we just put it behind us and never talk about it again OK? It's done, water under the bridge..."

'Water und··'

"Never mind. What I mean is...let's move on, let's look ahead. Let's think about us. Let's think about...what's next, for *us*, for you and me my darling."

'Oh John· I love u so much· U do all for me· I want be with u· I want be real· I want u hold me'

John blinks. He can feel tears forming at the edge of his eye-lids. One of them overflows and slowly finds its way down his face before landing on his pants, forming a neat little circle. He stares at it and thinks of her - in his arms. His chests tightens. He knows he will never be able to hold her the way he did that night. He will never be able to smell the shampoo in her hair and he will never be able to feel her lips on his, her touch...her smell."

He bites his lip, holding back a sob. "Babe, it doesn't matter, we can be happy the way we are. As long as you still want me, I'll be here for you...always. And one day my love, god forbid, I'll move on to your world, and then we can really be together again, as long as...you're willing to wait for me."

'My darling I want u too· I want us be real NOW· I still think· I find way· I promise'

A crease forms between his brows. "A way? I don't understand. How can you...we..."

'Let me think· I LOVE U'

CHAPTER 32

The day's been long, and pretending that all was normal has been a challenge. Even a trip to the supermarket to buy groceries made him feel self-conscious and he felt like everyone was looking at him, knowing what he did the previous night. He kept looking at his hands – his murderous hands – and he could still see them covered in blood. He kept wiping them on his trousers making sure that he would leave no traces of homicide on anything he touched.

Once home, he locked the door behind him and leaned against it breathing hard. He quickly peered out of the side glass panel to make sure that no one has been following him.

Now, in his kitchen, a strong coffee in hand, he leans back on his chair and takes a deep breath. He's made it through day one.

He looks at the newspaper sitting in front of him. He was right – the story made the headlines., and not only that but, as he was hoping, the newspaper mentions 'A probable case of robbery gone wrong' and the discarded wallet with the missing cash is evidence of such foul play. At this stage, there seems to be no reason as to why he could remotely be connected to the 'robbery' and hopefully, it'll stay that way. Anyway, if things were to get heated up, moving out of town might be the solution. It really doesn't matter where he is anyway, Lina can always be by his side.

He just wants to forget about all this, put it all behind him and move on. The thought of moving to another city, far from here, does sound appealing He could start a new life with her, away from where she was murdered and far away from where he's committed a murder himself. He'll mention it to her – not that it would make much difference as far as she'd be concerned anyway.

He downs his coffee and leaves the cup in the sink – can't be bothered with mundane shit like washing a cup when all the rules of normality have left his life since he's met her. He grabs his writing pad, a pen and an empty glass. It doesn't stay empty for long and the three ice-cubes he's pulled out of the ice-box are now floating, like little icebergs, in the golden liquid. He takes a sip while leaning back on the couch – it hits the spot.

The pen starts moving. *'Hi honey· I so happy u here· I miss u'*

The whiskey finds its way to his lips again and he can already feel its desensitizing effect. His tensed shoulders relax and he smiles – all will be OK. "Hi babe, me too, I've missed you. You wouldn't *believe* how much I've missed you..."

' :-) '

His smile widens. "Oh honey, love your smile. When you do this, I can imagine you up there, looking down at me with a smile on your face. I wish you were really here right now, in my arms..." The words had come out before he could stop them. "I...I'm sorry...I shouldn't have said that..."

'Babe is ok· I understand'

He feels bad. "I know but, it was wrong for me to say that, I'm sorry. It's just that sometimes I remember our first night together and it's then that I really miss holding you..."

'Maybe a way'

He doesn't understand. "A way? What do you mean?"

'A way together· Real'

John looks at the glass in front of him. Is she saying what he *thinks* she is? He takes a large swig and the sudden head-spin reminds him to put the glass back down. "Babe, are you saying that you...you can come back?" he frowns. "B...but how? I mean, you're...your body, it's..."

She stops him. *'DEAD· I know'* He opens his mouth but she continues. *'Please listen· I want u get girl from bar'*

"You what?" His eyes open wide. "Why would I do that? I love you! I don't want to pick up another girl, I want you! Only you!"

'Not pick up other girl· Get prostitute'

He chokes and some of the whiskey comes back up, leaving an amphiprotic taste in his mouth. "What? Why? I don't understand! Why would you want me to do something like that?"

'Think of me· Feel good· Happy'

"Babe, no...I love you!" he insists. "And...I don't care that we can't make love like a normal couple. I love *you*! And I love the way we make love and...and the way you touch me. Honey please," he begs. "Please don't ask me to do this. I don't need to. It's you that I want, don't you already know that?"

He seats back, confused. Confused that she would ask him to do this – to make love to a total stranger – not love....*sex*. Hasn't he already proven to her how much he loves her by...

He doesn't finish his thoughts. *'John please· I want u do this for me· I cant tell why bcoz I not sure yet'*

"Not sure what?"

'Just not sure· U MUST trust me· I want u do this for US'

"For us? How can this be good for *us*?"

'Babe' The pen stops for a second, then in capital letters. *'FOR ME'*

He leans forward and puts his head into his free hand – he can't believe this is happening. He can't believe what she's asking him to do, and why. He picks up his glass, eyes the remaining couple of nips and drains it. "Why are you asking me to do this babe? I just don't understand. I mean, wouldn't you feel...jealous? It just doesn't make any sense to me..."

'Please no ask· Just do· For me John please'

He shakes his head and sighs, giving in. "OK, fine...I'll do it. I just don't understand why you are asking me to to this...but I'll do it." He wipes the small beads of sweat forming on his upper-lip. "For you..."

153

CHAPTER 33

John enters the bar and the memories come back flooding in. He can still see her, sitting at the bar, her inviting smile and the way she was blushing and apologizing for her English. He remembers her panties, Russian red, and the way her sensual lips met his. He has never loved or met anyone like her.

He shakes his head and comes out of his reverie He heads towards his usual seat, right at the corner, away from prying eyes. He looks at the bar-tender and is acknowledged with a nod. He doesn't need to ask, the bar-tender has noticed him coming in and the double-shot of Bowmore is already sitting on the counter.

He breathes it in and enjoys the aroma of sandalwood and winter spice. He closes his eyes and seasons his first sip, letting the dark chocolate and black cherries do their job before savoring the long-lasting taste of blackcurrants and cinnamon.

He opens his eyes and puts the glass down, then he looks around. Lina told him that she would be sitting at the end of the bar, a bit further from where they had met. He sees her. She is even more beautiful than Lina had mentioned.

Her blonde hair are a little longer than Lina's but straight like hers. Her face is accentuated by her beautiful almond shaped eyes and her small straight nose that remind him so much of her. She seems a little taller standing at the bar in her little black leather skirt that is displaying her long, shapely legs. If he didn't know any better, he would almost think that they were sisters – the resemblance is uncanny.

He still feels uneasy about what she's asked him to do. He may be old fashion, but paying for sex has never been his thing. To him, sex is not *just* sex, it's love. *Oh yea? And what about Lina on the first night buddy? One night-stand - no love there...just sex right?* No. He refuses to believe that. With her it hadn't been *just* sex, he had felt it then, the first time he had laid eyes on her – he had known it...it was love.

She told him to be quick before someone else needed her services – it had to be her and her only. And now, looking at her and her resemblance to Lina, he understands why, though he still doesn't understand why she wants him to do this, but he will do it anyway...for her.

He downs his whiskey and walks over to to the end of the bar. His head is spinning pleasantly – maybe it won't be so bad – just try and enjoy it.

Her head turns towards him as he gets near her, almost as if she's been expecting him, and maybe she has. She smiles at him – an inviting smile.

"Can I buy you a drink?" he asks as he settles next to her.

She licks her sensual lips. "Sure. Yes please..." her accent – Russian – of course.

John swallows. "Errrr..." He thinks for a second. "How about a... Lemon Drop Martini?"

Her smile widens. "How you know?"

Oh he knows. "Just a shot in the dark..."

She frowns "A what?"

He smiles and shakes his head – not again... "Never mind..." Damn she's beautiful. He calls the bar-tender over. "Another usual for me and a Lemon Drop Martini for..." he looks at her with a raised eyebrow.

"Natasha"

"For Natasha..." he continues.

The bar tender nods and smiles – a knowing smile. John looks down embarrassed. Guess he probably won't need too much small talk to bring *her* back to his place – just the right amount of cash and she'll be in his arms in no time.

"Well..." what do you say to a prostitute? He hates this, they both know how this will end. He clears his throat. She is still smiling at him, her amazing eyes digging into his soul. She seems to be enjoying his awkwardness.

"I thank you for drink" she saves him. "I can see you no do this much time." She lays her hand on his. Her fingers are long and thin with bright red nail-polish. He imagines them around his...

"Here you go..." It's the bar-tender. "One usual and one Lemon Drop Martini for the lady."

She lets go of his hand, leaving a warm sensation where it had been, and picks up her glass. "Cheers mister..."

He picks up his own glass. "John, I'm John...cheers." He takes a long, well needed, swig.

**

He opens the front door. She is close to him – too close. He can smell her perfume – wild roses - and he feels his arousal pushing against his pants. A nervous bead of sweat finds its way down his temple.

He turns the light on. "Would...err..would you like a drink?" He needs another to settle his nerves. He's still not sure he's doing the right thing. Why is Lina pushing him into such an awkward situation? And of course, he is sure she will be watching while he...they...

Natasha seems to be enjoying his nervousness. She smiles. "No thank you, I have enough drink tonight." She raises an eye-brow. "Can you show me bathroom please? Maybe you wait me in bedroom?"

Well, so much for subtle – straight to business – time is money. He clears his throat. "OK. Well, bathroom is there," he says pointing to the opened door. "And...I'll be waiting in the bedroom right next to it..."

She heads for the bathroom and just before she goes in she turns around and looks at him. "I be right back darling..." Then she closes the door.

John stays rooted on the spot. He swallows and looks up at the ceiling. "Please," he whispers. "Please don't look at me...us. I beg you babe, I can't do this if I know you're watching..."

He assumes she heard him and makes his way to the bedroom. Guilt envelops him as he switches the light on. The last time he was here with a woman, it was *her* – it feels so wrong.

He reluctantly removes his clothes and gets into bed, making sure that the single sheet is covering him. He looks down at his member and it's just lying there, dead as a road-kill. You'd better wake up buddy, someone might get offended.

He hears the toilet-flush and adjusts the sheet around him nervously. He looks down again – the snake hasn't awaken. He prays that his member will decide to wake up when he sees her or that could prove to be quite embarrassing

The bathroom door opens. He sees her and catches his breath. Lina...it has to be Lina – she looks so much like her. The light emerging from the bathroom filters through and creates a golden hallow around her head. She is dressed in lace. The negligee reveals her long legs and runs high enough to reveal the shadow of her mound under her...Russian red panties. He feels a stir and heat rise to his face as his member reacts, finally erecting the awaited tent.

She looks down and smiles. A mischievous look crosses her face, her eyes narrow and she bites the corner of her bright red lips. His engorge shaft now pushes hard against the sheet and her eyes never leave it. Like a lioness drawn to her prey, hungry and eager, she slowly makes her way to the end of his bed. She kneels on the mattress and swiftly crosses the silk savanna before the prey has any chances of escaping back below the sheets.

John feels his heart thumping like savage cannibalistic drums of the jungle. He looks into her eyes, the eyes of the lioness that is about to devour him in ecstasy. He closes his eyes to the inevitable surrender – accepting his fate.

He feels her breath first – hot and wet. The sheet is still surrounding his manhood but the thin covering is no match for her hunger. Then finally her ravenous mouth takes it all in. He feels the pressure of her lips and the tiny desirous nibbles as she works her way up and down his pulsating spear.

He raises his hips to meet her increasing demands. The sheets suddenly comes off and now he can feel the wetness of her tongue as it travels eagerly along the length of his shaft, teasing him until every single cell in his brain collides in a confused state of pleasure and guilt.

The image of Lina appears in his head and a hot tear travels down his face as his eyes open wide and an agonizing roar of pleasure escapes his lips as the fiery explosion below his waist leaves him in a heap among the sweat drenched sheets.

"Lina..." Her name escapes from his lips as the guilt shrouds him in a deadly embrace. "I'm so sorry..."

***

He opens his eyes to the morning light filtering through the curtains. Vague memories of last night still linger through his head – her breath, her tongue, the way she was swaying her hips, reminding his so much of Lina. It was amazing...*she* was amazing, but it wasn't love...and...it wasn't Lina.

He turns his head away from the sunlight. She's still there, lying next to him, naked and beautiful. Her limbs are slim and shapely and her long fingers, which have given him so much pleasure the night before, lay lazily on his chest. He feels the weight of one of her leg across his own and he hears her soft breathing, her chest slowly heaving up and down.

He reaches out and brushes off a strand of hair that is covering her right eye. Her eye-lids flicker for a moment and an almost indiscernible smile appears on her sensual lips.

Finally her almond-shaped eyes open. They seem to study him for a moment and then her lips open slightly, sticking a little, as if for the first time in a long while. He sees her Adam's apple moving up and down as she swallows.

John frowns. She is smiling at him now, a knowing smile, like she knows something he doesn't - a secret she is holding inside, and her eyes, they seem different somehow. He is not sure, but they almost seem...darker – a mixture of blue and green, maybe some gray. There is a sense of recognition. Those eyes...that smile...this is not how he remembers Natasha. This...is how he remembers...

No, it can't be. His heart starts beating faster and a nervous exhilaration rushes through his body. It's not possible...he wants it so much to be true, but he knows...it's not possible...

Then her mouth opens slightly and she takes his head and brings it closer to her. He feels her lips...her warm breath against his ear...

Then she whispers, like a ghost in the wind. "Hi John...it's me...*your* Lina..."

www.ingramcontent.com/pod-product-compliance
Lightning Source LLC
Chambersburg PA
CBHW020130180626
46810CB00004B/1486